COMHAIRLE CHONTAE ÁTHA CLIATH THEAS

SOUTH DUBLIN COUNTY LIBRARIES

COUNTY LIBRARY, TOWN CENTRE, TALLAGHT
TO RENEW ANY ITEM
OR ONLINE AT www.southdublinlibraries.ie

Items should be returned on or before the last date below. Fines, as displayed in the Library, will be charged on overdue items.

CAPTAIN

Sam Angus was born in Italy, grew up in France and Spain, and was educated rather haphazardly in most of these countries, at many different schools. She studied English Literature at Trinity College, Cambridge, where she kept a dog until he was discovered being smuggled out of college in a laundry basket. She taught A level English before spending a decade in the fashion industry and now writes full time.

She lives between Exmoor and London with improvident numbers of children, dogs and horses.

CAPTAIN

SAM ANGUS

MACMILLAN CHILDREN'S BOOKS

First published 2014 by Macmillan Children's Books
a division of Macmillan Publishers Limited
20 New Wharf Road, London N1 9RR
Basingstoke and Oxford
Associated companies throughout the world
www.panmacmillan.com

ISBN 978-1-4472-6302-9

1 3 5 7 9 8 6 4 2

A CIP catalogue record for this book is available from
the British Library.

Printed and bound by CPI Group (UK) Ltd, Croydon CR0 4YY

For Harley

Don't walk behind me, I may not lead.
Don't walk in front of me, I may not follow.
Just walk beside me and be my friend.

Albert Camus

FOREWORD

December 1918

I dictate the lines you now read from a hospital bunk in Cairo, a few each day, or as many as Nurse has time for.

The bullet I tempted never got me. In the end only splinters of hot metal had my number. In the hectic, hollow days leading up to Damascus, I watched with reckless curiosity as my wound turned from red to green. I had tempted every bullet, but my life seemed charmed and it was only small splinters of hot metal that found their mark in me.

Now, a little each day, I relive the moments that give me no peace, and I dredge into this cruel desert light the memories, which are more blistering than any fever, more cankerous than the sepsis on my arm: the memories of a friend lost. I wince and cover my eyes, but I'm almost done. I was always clumsy with words, but my memory is good and I speak as honestly as I can bring myself to. Some of my friend's story I've guessed at, some he told me, in his strange, reluctant English.

Nurse is kind to me. Her pen moves across the page and she betrays no horror, neither has she yet put down her pen or walked away. She raises her eyes to me, but I cannot read her thoughts, and her pen moves on across the page – I thank her for that and hope that you too, reader, will hear me out.

PART I

EGYPT

Alexandria

August 1915

It was in Egypt that I saw Captain for the first time. The others had gone out drinking at the Cap d'Or Café, determined to live it up on our last night. I wandered out, feeling very alone, with no friend to go to but the horses, the men's mockery still pinching a raw nerve. I was the youngest of us all by a long chalk and I took their ragging and teasing the wrong way. I had no whiskers to shave and didn't drink, so I'd toyed with my knife, wanting it to look as though I wasn't going to the Cap d'Or because there was still jam and bread on my plate.

'Come on, boy,' Lieutenant Straker had called. The Strakers had the Manor House at Bredicot back home. All of us Bayliss boys and Mother were a little in awe of Lady Straker, so I wished I were not in his platoon and that he wasn't so familiar and joshing with me. It made me uncomfortable, what with him being a Second Lieutenant and his family being neighbours and him probably knowing my age, and anyway, I'd never had a drink.

'Have a beer, Billy,' Firkins said, then Merrick and Robins and Tandy and all of them joined in too.

'Have a beer, Billy, come on, have a beer.'

Until the Lieutenant said, 'Leave the boy alone. What does it matter to us if he doesn't drink?'

That morning too, when he was shaving, Robins laughed at me and called me 'girlie', and it had been just like the schoolroom at Bredicot again when I'd stood with Abel Rudge and the others, before Divinity, measuring our chests with wooden rulers to work out our chances of being recruited. None of us were old enough, not by a long way, but Rudge had said to pick cards to see who'd try for it. I'd turned up the knave of clubs, and Rudge had smirked and said, 'It's Billy, little Billy Bayliss's going to have a try.'

So I did have a try, you see – none of us Bayliss boys likes to let a challenge go by – and in the end it'd all been easy, being recruited. I'd half-inched my brother Francis's papers and left Bredicot. We'd lined up at the town hall, there'd been other boys there from school too in that queue, and we'd been stripped and examined, and I'd stood in line, standing up tall and wide as I could, trying to add two years to my chest to make me look Francis's seventeen.

'Put on your clothes. You'll do.'

There were three of us Bayliss boys – Francis, Geordie and me – and no one could tell us apart.

6

Francis had the right number of years, but bad feet, so I was all right and I passed muster, but none of the other boys from school did.

A Sergeant-Major had formed us into fours and marched us to the race track and I spent that night on a cement floor, wedged between lines of fold-up seats, trousers wrapped round our boots for a pillow.

I felt guilty about leaving home but I thought more about Abel Rudge's surprise when he knew I'd got through than I did about Mother. With Father gone, things were a bit tight at home and she'd find it easier with one less.

When the training was over and we boarded the *Saturnia*, the others had stowed their kit in the steerage quarters, then rushed up to the poop deck to wave goodbye to their families, but there'd been no one on the wharf to see me off. There had been a parcel, though, from Mother, just before we'd entrained for Avonmouth. In it was a pair of field glasses and a note.

Dear Billy,
I understand you are now 17 and for your unexpected coming of age I thought these field glasses might come in useful. They were your father's.

Billy, I know there's no point trying to stop you. I've always said there's no point trying to stop a Bayliss. You are all just like your father – you more than any of them – and there was never any stopping him.

Good luck, Billy.

Love, Mother.

I'd stayed below deck watching through a tight and greasy window as England ebbed away. She was always practical and brisk, Mother, in her letters, in everything really, as unfussing a sort of person as you could find anywhere.

There'd been no peace on the *Saturnia*, the food vile, the hammocks cheek by jowl, the heat fierce. We'd passed the snow-tipped mountains of southern Spain and the Algerian coast. No one knew where we were headed. 'Smyrna,' Robins said, and I'd taken little notice, such whispers changing as they did with each wind. We heard we were stopping at Alexandria and Lieutenant Straker said, 'It'll be Gallipoli then.' Firkins told me in front of all the men that Gallipoli was the rocky tail-end of Europe, a place of myth and legend. It was embarrassing in front of the men, the way Firkins always spoke to me as if I were in a History lesson. He could speak through a corner of his mouth without removing the pipe that was always clamped in there, even when he didn't have any tobacco to put in it.

We'd waited a long time in Egypt. We'd marched in sand and eaten sand till I was sick of the stuff. I'd seen the men who came back from Gallipoli – they'd been Australians, mostly, big, well-made men. We'd unloaded them on the docks, the dead in the same tubs as the living, the green flies on their yellow-black wounds. But some of them joshed and asked for beers even as they lay there with their wounds all maggoty or their legs blown off.

Now I knew I was going to the place those men had come from and I was scared.

I was relieved, though, to be leaving Egypt, where I'd felt so alone. There were men in Egypt from all over the place: Indians, Gurkhas, Australians, Tommies, New Zealanders, Maoris, Sikhs, Frenchmen, and negroes from all our colonies, but I'd found no friend among them all. Somehow being in the army made me feel young and scared when I'd thought I'd feel manly and grown up. Living amongst men like Merriman and Merrick and all just made me more aware of the difference that the years make.

That last night in Egypt, as I walked towards the horse lines, the sun set and turned the sky to violet, and the sand to the pink of a Worcestershire apple. The sweetnesss of all that rosy light made me think of Bredicot. I'd write to Liza, I thought, because she'd keep a secret. I was the favourite of her brothers. She would've minded my going most, and I could remind her again how Trumpet was fond of apples and small wild strawberries and of being scratched behind the ears.

9

I stopped and turned. The lights of the camp were all twinkling and magical as fairyland, and I thought how I could tell Liza about our new issue of tropical kit: light shorts, shirts open at the throat, sleeves rolled up. I could tell her what fine men the Worcester Yeomanry were and that she'd read about us in the papers but I wouldn't tell her that I was going to Gallipoli, nor that we were leaving our horses behind. I was worried, you see, that I wouldn't look so good, to Liza or to Abel Rudge, now that I was going to fight on foot.

I don't remember everything clearly, or the days, or the order in which things happened later, but what happened next I remember as if it were yesterday. I walked on through the balmy Egyptian night, over the moonlit sand, past where the Gurkhas liked to fish with string and bamboo canes, past the natives loading and unloading, past rows of khaki tents and towards the transport lines.

There were all sorts in the transport lines, mules and what have you, but I never so much as looked at them as I passed. A horse man is a horse man and won't look at anything other than a horse, so I never gave the mules and suchlike a second thought.

I found the Yeomanry horse section and wandered idly from one horse to another. None of them stamped softly or snorted when I came to them in the way that Trumpet would, but I was glad Trumpet was at Bredicot with Liza and hadn't crossed the sea in the stinking belly of a troopship, only to be abandoned here to the sand and flies.

I leaned against the neck of a tall bay horse that I liked the look of and blew into his nostrils. He lowered his head to me but didn't close his eyes at the blowing, like Trumpet would. As I leaned there and heard the cosy snuffling of horses and looked up into the strangely close, swaying eastern stars, I breathed the peace of a desert night.

I stroked the bay, feeling sorry that there was no grass in all of Egypt for him, but he snatched his head from me and gazed ahead, over the top of the long-eared mules, surveying, in the far-sighted way of all horses, the distance. The horses – not one of them – so much as acknowledged the presence of the mules who were right in front of them, mules and suchlike being so far below their own dignity.

I waited for the bay to drop his head to my hand again.

There was a noise somewhere beneath the palm trees: a man's voice raised in anger. Closer at hand, in the mule lines, there was a sudden darting shadow. The bay threw his head and whinnied. I glimpsed a slight figure, a boy, slim and naked to the waist, a pair of dark eyes, the whites of them bright as moons.

In the second that our eyes met, each assessed the other and knew, immediately and instinctively, that we were, there or thereabouts, the same age. He glanced towards the palms, then back to me. Eyes wide and imploring, he raised a finger to his lips. He dropped his hand to the neck of the animal immediately in front of me and whispered to it. I looked at it for the first time, saw how its silver ears were longer than those of the other mules, and beautifully marked with dark wavering edges, as wobbly as if the boy, in some lonely quiet moment, had once inked in those tips, because they had a sweet, uncertain line to them, as though put there by the hand of a child. It was smaller than the others, too; a donkey perhaps. It brayed: a smiling sort of bark, merry and loud for so small a creature. The boy flinched, shied, like a wild animal. He ducked under the neck of the silver donkey and into the shadow.

A breeze rustled the palm leaves and I heard the man's voice again, still loud and angry. Two men stood beneath the flickering palms, one a Major, the other a Sergeant. The bay tensed and pricked his ears. He was like Trumpet, I thought: a horse who missed nothing, a horse full of heart; not at all the sort to eat while grown men argued and young boys hid. I scratched him. He nuzzled me then swung his head away.

The Major stretched out his arms and tore at the stripes on the Corporal's arm. I heard a stifled whimper and turned: there was the boy – clutching at a young palm, a hand raised to his mouth.

'Sir, I do what you say, I do – I do everything you say,' said the Corporal in halting English. 'It was not me who stole the grain, sir . . .' He wore standard British service dress, the stripes of a Corporal on his arm, but his cap badge was a star within three circles and his voice was thick and foreign.

The boy dropped his head, fear outlined in the dark cringing curve of his shadow on the white sand.

'Not me, sir . . .'

'I trusted you.'

The boy recoiled. I could see his face and glistening eyes. He turned and made as if to intervene, just as the Major, in a surge of anger, lurched towards the Corporal. The boy shrank back.

'Damn you, Thomas, damn you for your thieving, you . . . Damn you – after all I've done!'

The Major grabbed the Corporal's arm and tore at the cloth of his sleeve. Explosive with rage and irritation at the stubborn cloth, the Major wrenched and pulled till he had what he wanted.

'You're lucky it's just your stripes I'm taking . . .' The Major hurled the torn stripes down and ground them into the muck of the horse lines with his heel.

The Corporal's face was wide with shock, eyes rheumy, arms outstretched.

'And you're lucky it's just this.' The Major's heels swivelled again, as if to murder the cloth. 'The official punishment for larceny . . .' He thought better of whatever he was going to threaten, said, 'Damn you, Thomas!' then turned and swung furiously away.

The Corporal bent and nodded his head: once, very slowly, twice, then a third time.

The bay tossed and neighed. A good horse dislikes argument between men and I put a hand to his cheek to soothe him. The Corporal's head sank lower still. He remained bent and bowed for a long while, the boy and I waiting and watching, separately and secretly.

When the Corporal raised his head, he turned to the mule lines, paused, then went straight away to the silvery donkey in front of my horse, and stood at the creature's side a while, the boy staying hidden only feet away.

'Hey-Ho,' the Corporal whispered. 'Hey-Ho.' And there was the sadness of all the centuries in his whispering. He raised one hand to his arm, to where the stripes had been, fingers trembling there.

'My friend,' he said. 'The Major was once my friend.' He bent his head to the donkey's neck and said, 'Hey-Ho, even for you I would not steal.'

Something caught the old man's eye and dragged him from his reverie. He moved to the nosebag and checked it, surprise dawning on his wide face. He cast around, moved on to the next animal. Again he stopped, scratched his head, weighed the nosebag in his hand, and went to the next, and so on, checking the knot and weight of each. He turned and walked back again along the line, again touching each animal, each bag.

'Strange . . . strange . . . all done.' He puzzled. He stopped and shook his head at the mystery of things, then the old man, for old he seemed to me, turned and walked, still shaking his head, till he was lost in the frond shadow.

After a minute or two, the boy crept towards the patch of sand on which the men had stood. His father was in the Army, I thought, watching, but the boy wasn't because he had no badge, no tunic. He crouched and picked up the torn cloth, shook off the dirt and sand, wiped it on his knees, wiped again, smoothed it and lifted it to his streaked cheeks.

'Father . . .' he whispered. 'Father, Apa, it was me . . .' His voice melted into the sigh of the wind and I didn't catch any more.

After a little while, he rose and went to the donkey and laid his head on the grey back.

'I will stay with you, Hey-Ho, with you and with Apa. I will look after you both, Hey-Ho. Better.'

I waited an instant, then stepped forward.

'Hello.'

He started, for he must've forgotten I was there.

'I'm Billy,' I said, and stuck out my hand in a very English sort of manner. He flinched and shrank away.

'You're not in the Army, are you?' I said.

He started, now doubly wary. I looked at his swollen eyes and the smears of dust and tears on his cheeks.

'Because if you were in the Army, you wouldn't cry. You never cry, however much you want to.'

At this he paused and searched my face, running his eyes over my uniform. He made an almost imperceptible movement with his head: difficult to say if it were a yes or a no.

'You have Hey-Ho,' I said. 'I wish I had my horse.'

He looked up at me briefly, then dropped his eyes to Hey-Ho, his fingers tracing the black rim of an ear.

'Hey-Ho's bark is like a smile or a laugh,' I said, because I could see the tenderness of the gesture and wanted to say something nice about Hey-Ho. 'But his eyes are so sad . . .'

The boy looked up again then, and he was steady and serious when he said, 'They have seen too many terrible things . . .'

His own eyes, too, I knew, must've seen those terrible things, but I didn't ask then what they were.

'I must look after him,' he said. 'After Hey-Ho and after Father.' He put a hand on Hey-Ho, and the donkey answered loudly with that joyous laughter running in his *hee-haw*.

'Hey-Ho? Why Hey-Ho?' I asked, amused by the quaint Englishness of the name tongued in the boy's foreign voice.

'They told me . . . where I come from . . . that

English donkeys go *Hey-Ho*.' His voice hee-hawed up and down as he said it. 'All other donkeys go *Hee-haw*.' His face was so solemn that I had to laugh. He looked more puzzled at that, and I was still laughing when I asked, 'Is he an English donkey?'

'We will go to England, one day, Father says, so we called him Hey-Ho.'

I was still laughing but he was still puzzled, so I put on a straight face and asked, 'What is your name?'

His limbs seemed to coil, as if he were readying himself to spring away. I caught him by the arm, wanting him to stay, this boy, with whom I didn't have to pretend I was not scared, from whom I did not have to hide tears.

'What's your name?' I asked again.

He studied me again, as if deciding whether to answer. When he spoke it was in his strange, faltering English.

'Before . . . before . . . my name was Benjamin . . . Here, they call me Captain. The English Major, he used to call me Captain.'

As if regretting he'd said so much, he tugged his arm away, sprang to his feet and sped away, barefoot and silent on the sand.

Alexandria

14 August 1915

We Yeomen left the next morning while it was still dark, in silence but for the tramping of so many feet. By the time the sun was high we were in the seething stench and filth of Alexandria.

We halted to let a column of horses by, the men in files of threes, each man leading two mounts. I thought of Trumpet again as I watched them go by and felt glad he was not here in apple-less Egypt.

A troop of old soldiers pushed past us, laughing at the shine and polish of our kit, at the weight of it. We marched on through the quaint white streets and their pushing press of humanity and the jangle of foreign tongues. Arab hawkers swarmed round us, crying out their whining chants.

The dock was immense, forty quays or more, an Armada of vessels of all kinds in it – destroyers, troopships, cruisers, liners, hospital ships. Provisions stood in stacks on every quay: ammunition, water-cans, crates and tins. Everywhere were trains of horses, gun limbers, field kitchens; officers calling out, still recruiting men; lines of sick and wounded soldiers in blue hospital uniforms.

'Gallipoli,' Sparrow said, pointing to a row of wounded. 'They're from Gallipoli.'

I felt a tightening of the heart, the cold fingers of fear. Did no man leave Gallipoli standing? Was it only the dead or the near-dead that got out? There were only men with whiskers here, men who didn't mind the yellow wounds and the burned flesh melded to khaki cloth. I was alone, very alone, among such men. What would Abel Rudge feel, I wondered if he'd seen those men from Gallipoli, would he be scared too? Yes, I was too young; if I told Lieutenant Straker my age, I could go home to Bredicot. That boy from last night, had he seen what men looked like when they came back from Gallipoli? How would he feel in my place? How would he feel if he were going to Gallipoli?

If only he were with us, there'd be at least someone else to talk to.

We halted beside two large ships: the *Anglo-Egyptian* and the *Ascania*. Behind us stood a great dock-shed, the side of it open to the harbour. I smelt the mules before I saw them – a mule makes an unholy stink compared to a horse, especially in the heat of Egypt. I looked into the dock-shed and glimpsed, behind the stores and equipment, three lines of pack-animals. Hey-Ho – was he in there?

'Bayliss – into line!'

I stepped back and waited in file as steep gangways were placed to the lowest deck of the *Anglo-Egyptian*. Still we waited and while we waited, I wondered about the mules and wondered if the boy – Captain he'd said he was known as – if Captain were with them. Further down the quay, a bit of a palaver was going on, an officer trying to get sixty-odd stubborn transport horses up the gangway on to a battleship called the *Pasha*. A chestnut mare was walking peacefully up, neat as ninepence, her nose calmly in her nosebag but halfway up, she stopped dead. She raised her head and pulled at the rope, every line of her firm in the determination to go no further. I smiled, thinking how Trumpet would do just the same if I were to bring him to a filthy Egyptian dock and force him up a narrow gangplank. Behind the mare, horses were whinnying and pulling back. Two subalterns, red-faced and ruffled, were whipping the mare's rump. We were all laughing then at the subalterns, but at the same time I knew I'd not want to be behind her on that plank if she kicked or reared.

We waited in the hot sun. I was standing near John Merriman, Ernest Sparrow, Archie Spade and Harry Beasley, half listening to their talk about the Turks and their fear of a bayonet, half thinking of the night before, of Captain's secrecy and stealth, wondering what lay behind it, wondering about his attachment to Hey-Ho. What were the terrible things the donkey's eyes had seen? I smiled to myself at the notion of all the English donkeys that said 'Hey-ho, hey-ho'.

'They say the Turk dislikes our bayonets.' Merriman was grinning. 'They say he's scared of a hand-to-hand fight.' Then Firkins started going on about how we were off to a great and tragic battlefield, a land of romance and myth, the land of Dionysius and Ariadne and Jason and all the others. Beasley and Spade groaned and rolled their eyes.

Old Colonel Colville ordered us into the dock-shed. The Colonel was from somewhere around Bredicot. He'd been a contemporary of Father's, I think, maybe a friend too, the name being familiar to me. Both Lieutenant Straker and the Colonel made me uncomfortable, and there were times I wished I hadn't joined a Worcestershire Regiment, it all being so sort of close to home if you were under-age. Dixies of sugary tea and greasy bacon from the Tommy cookhouse on the dock were handed round.

'Lead out the mules!' someone ordered.

I stood a little apart from the others, watching as each mule was led out, but they were all short-eared, run-of-the-mill-looking things.

'They go below,' Lieutenant Straker said, joining me. 'In the stalls below the officers' horses.'

The mules were tied in slings alongside the *Ascania*.

'Lieutenant, sir, do you know . . .' I began hesitantly.

'Are the mules coming with us?'

All the usual shenanigans and kerfuffle were going on, the biting and the kicking and the whole palaver that you get when you tie an innocent, unsuspecting quadruped up in a sling and whisk it twenty foot off the ground into an ocean-bound ship.

The Lieutenant answered, grinning, 'Looks as though they have their own view on the matter.'

I'd wanted to ask if he knew of Captain, but how could you ask after someone if you didn't even know his surname and he wasn't in the Army?

'First Yeomanry, prepare to board!' growled old Colonel Colville.

I smiled at Merrick's reluctant, mocking salute, his teasing imitation of the accent of the commanding classes. I wouldn't want to be the Turk that faced his bayonet, or Spade's, or Beasley's, or the Lieutenant's, such a tight, strong-looking bunch they were, proud and fierce and caring only for their own. Lieutenant Straker seemed old to me then. He wasn't older than the other men, but there was an angry kind of courage in him and a natural authority.

We emerged into the white light of the midday sun.

'First Yeomanry, board the *Ascania*.'

She was the ship the mules had boarded, but I'd not seen Hey-Ho, so Captain would most likely not be on the *Ascania* either. I sighed, feeling tired of living up to men like Merriman and Beasley and Spade, tired of trying to be jolly about bayonets, tired of having no one around with whom I could be myself.

That first day aboard the *Ascania* we started training in the use of a bayonet. A bayonet is a different thing altogether to a rifle. I thought I could fire at a man with a rifle, but I didn't know then if I could ever kill a man with a bayonet.

'Go in with the point,' Colonel Colville told us.

As I stood there on the hot deck, the bayonet in hand, I looked at Merrick's face, and Beasley's, and Sparrow's but they, none of them, seemed to quail at the idea of going in with the point.

I'm fifteen, I thought as I fixed the bayonet. Only fifteen, and I will have to kill men. I have to go in with the point and I have to kill. I will kill or I will be killed.

The Colonel must've seen something on my face, because he marched up to me and barked, 'Get this into your head! This is war, and the only thing that'll count out there is that you win and that you stay alive. Make sure it's the enemy that dies and not you.'

The days were hot and slow. A bugle woke us at six for breakfast, we drilled on deck from nine to eleven, then in the height of the day, struck senseless with the force of the sun, the boards of the *Ascania* blistering, the colour stolen from the sea, we were allowed to rest. Everyone else had a mucker, someone to play cards with or chat to. I would always be on my own then. No one said so, but they knew I was younger. Lieutenant Straker almost certainly had some idea, but I don't think, now, looking back, that he ever breathed a word to anyone.

One such afternoon, I lay on my own on the shadowy side of the deck and thought about the bayonets. Merrick had taken me aside after the training that day and told me the easy part was the pushing it in, that a bayonet sticks in a stomach and is hard to pull out, that you have to twist it and tug. Then the others had laughed when they'd seen my face – they'd all been laughing at me. I'd never thought of any of this in the Bredicot schoolroom – of bayonet wounds, nor of the twist of steel in a stomach – and wondered if Abel Rudge or Francis could kill a man in hand-to-hand combat. I wasn't sure. Perhaps it was easier to kill a man if you were older. My thoughts drifted then to Captain. I'd begun to wonder, you see, by then, if he'd been only the melting figment of my lonely mind, for there'd been no sign of him nor Hey-Ho since that night in the horse lines in Egypt.

I stretched my arms out, inspecting my tanned skin. We'd marched ten times around the first-class deck that morning, two and a half miles in all, to the beat of the band, the brassy thump of the sun on our backs and the ships from all the oceans of the world going about on either side.

At Bredicot, when I felt most alone, I'd always go to

Trumpet and the other horses. That afternoon, too, I left the deck and crept below to the officers' horses. They were all jammed together in restless lines – no air, no room to exercise or groom them. Somewhere one was thrashing, rearing and striking at the wood with his forelegs. Men were shouting, the horse smashing against his stall, a vet trying to calm him, then taking a needle to him. I crept away, nauseous with the heat, and the swell of the sea, and the stink. I longed for the companionship of Trumpet as there's no finer friend than a horse when you're lonely, but was glad really that I hadn't brought him with me to the burning bowels of the *Ascania*, to be driven mad with the heat.

I left and went down the steep gangways: two decks down was where the mules were kept. I searched the lines stall by stall, just in case I'd missed Hey-Ho before, but they were all ordinary-looking things, no long black-tipped ears.

The sunset was a melancholy thing, all purples and greens and chromes, and I felt lonelier for its loveliness. Hour after hour, I watched the wash of the water along the bow, gazed at all the tiny passing islands of the Greek Aegean, all strung out, till I was almost hypnotized by the hiss of the bow wave. It grew dark and I set to tramping up and down the deck with my tinful of thick, sugary tea. The boards were wet with dew beneath my bare feet, the touch of the breeze sweet and soft on my bare skin, those strange, eastern stars above. I heard Merrick and the others laughing like drains at something or other, and I wished Liza were with me, or Francis, or almost anyone.

A hospital ship passed, her green starboard light burning in the dark. Our own portholes were darkened, and we crossed her like a shadow, dark and silent, the captaincy wary, watching to the left and to the right for what might lie below.

The *Ascania* steered around two tiny islets, turned, and navigated a passage deep between two great hills into the harbour of Moudros. A grey destroyer drew up alongside, her sailors all waving their caps at us, her band playing us in. At anchor there were cruisers, destroyers, mine-sweepers, mine-layers, hospital ships, launches, submarines – a terrific spirit-stirring display of sea power. Francis would have liked to see this, I thought. He had a collection of lead ships in his room at Bredicot. On the hills above the bay, white tents seemed to have bloomed like desert roses, each one fluttering with an ensign or hospital cross or French tricolour.

There at Moudros, pinnaces and packet boats dashed around in all directions day and night. The right food or equipment was always on the wrong boat; there were no water carts on the shore, no kettles, cookers, or signalling equipment to be had anywhere. We Yeomanry were to sleep aboard the

Ascania, Colonel Colville told us, our departure for Gallipoli being so imminent, but we were kept there in the harbour for three days practising going up and down the rope ladders they dropped over the sides of the ship. On the third day the Lieutenant sent me ashore on some errand or other so I got a break from all the climbing up and climbing down.

After the errand I had time to spare and reckoned I wouldn't be missed for a while, so, for the joy of being on solid land again, I walked over the sun-scorched grass between the hospital tents and on upwards. The heat was as fierce as the blast from a furnace but there was a village up there ahead, gleaming white in the hollow of a hill and it might've been that, or the fear of what might happen in the days to come, that made me want to climb that hill. At the top, I told myself, there'd be a view, perhaps, and I might see Gallipoli. I climbed past the village and on, then sat there at the top and caught my breath and wiped my streaming face and fought away the flies. The sheep bells echoed across the still water of the bay and all the great ships down there looked like tiny painted toys. Across the sea somewhere lay Gallipoli. I scanned the horizon. Far away, through a quivering violet haze, I saw what looked like a whale-backed hump in the silvery surface of the sea. The tail-end of Europe. Gallipoli. I raised Father's field glasses to my eyes. I was rather proud of them, and took them everywhere, because in the

Army only the officers are given glasses.

I caught, or thought I caught, a distant pulsing in the air. I started and tensed and wiped the glasses and looked again. My fingers trembled on the field glasses. That throbbing, that pulsing was the sound of guns: the guns of Gallipoli.

The heat fell away. The buzzing of the flies quieted and still I stared towards that blue-grey ridge; was still staring as the sun sank in a blaze, blood-red and pink. I thought wistfully how that sun would soon set too on the hills of Worcestershire. In two hours it would be sundown at home, and the throbbing of those guns, the fear of what lay ahead, made me long to hang on to the reins of the sun and be galloped westward on her rays, to Bredicot.

The end of the day was bugled, and the call taken up from camp to camp. Then the French trumpets began their wailing and the mournful cries echoed up to the tops of the hill and soon it seemed that the whole island was crying out the sad news of the sun's setting once again. I watched the dusty mules nibble at scorched thistles, listened to the wailing of the trumpets and the ringing of the sheep bells, and felt lonelier then than I'd ever felt, and smaller. When the first campfire was lit I started on down, slipping on the loose stones that glowed rose-pink in the last of the sun's rays.

Merrick and Firkins were there on the dock.

'Young Bayliss, you'll get it in the neck,' hissed Merrick. 'Where've you been? There'll be the devil to pay – the Lieutenant's been looking for you.'

'We're under orders to proceed to the peninsula. Tonight,' said Firkins, very solemn and portentous. 'History is in the making, young Bayliss.' He removed his pipe to illustrate the importance of the moment. 'The dawn of a new chapter.' His cap was adrift, his tunic all wrongly buttoned and he didn't look at all like the dawn of a new chapter, but I felt a tremor of fear. By morning I would be at Gallipoli. By morning I would see action for the first time.

We worked to breaking point on the dock, Firkins and Merrick and Beasley and I, loading stack after stack of provisions. The bay was all feverish commotion: forage, equipment, ammunition, mules, all being moved from jetties to barges, trawlers towing strings of rowboats to the ships. Hour after hour, boatload after boatload of troops were ferried to the ships, till there was moonshine on the water and the ships all twinkling with their strings of red and green lights and the bands all playing on the warships and the tom-toms beating from the Indian camps.

'Embark at once. Board the *Queen Victoria*.'

The order was passed mouth to mouth, along the jetty. I lifted the last crate of many hundreds labelled 'Medical Supplies' on to a lighter, and looked up to watch a liner steam out of the bay, her band playing a rousing air and every vessel at anchor waving as she disappeared into the dark of the open sea.

Firkins and I squeezed ourselves on to a barge and found a place to sit between the crates of medical supplies. We crossed the flickering water in eerie silence, dark forms gliding to and fro in the balmy night.

As we rounded the stern of the *Victoria*, I saw a pair of mules being hustled into a sling. They were making their usual song and dance about the whole thing, protesting and kicking and yanking and biting and the whole shebang. They were suddenly whistled off their hoofs and hoisted, still and silent with shock, their four hoofs dangling, then swung and plunged on to the deck.

Merrick looked up at the moon and frowned, then Beasley and Sparrow did, and one by one, each man looked up at her. She was bright and full and her light would be no friend to us that night. A tot was passed hand to hand, from bow to stern.

'Young Billy,' said Merrick, passing it to me, and there was amusement and challenge in his eyes, so I, in a spurt of defiance, lifted it to my lips and swallowed, and the shock of the stuff in my throat was burning and violent.

As the tug that had held the mules prepared to pull away, a dark figure sprang from the stern of the last boat, leaped to the rope ladder and pulled swiftly up.

I leaped to my feet – the boy – Captain! A *stowaway?* I forced my way along the deck between the crates, through the Lovat Scouts, the Yeomanry, the Essex, and all the different sorts that were in the barge, to the front. When we were finally alongside, I was the first off the barge, the first to scale the ladder up the *Victoria*, climbing hastily and clumsily, my pack lurching and swinging. I searched the top deck, the deck below, the deck below that, then deeper still to the mule lines. I was quiet and went on tiptoe, keeping to the places where there was straw on the ground because Captain didn't want to be seen, didn't want to be found.

A shadow moved fleetingly on the ceiling somewhere, but when I stopped to listen there was only the familiar breathing and chomping and shuffling of the animals.

There was a loud *hee-haw*, and another. I heard the laugh running through those hee-haws, so I knew them straight away for Hey-Ho's. I waited, and after a while picked out, amidst the shuffling hoofs, the wincing scrape of metal on metal. I moved along the line, past one mule after another – all run-of-the-mill things, short-eared and plain as pikestaffs. From tail to tail I went, all the way to the stern of the *Victoria*, and there – there it was again, louder, the clink of a shovel on an iron-clad floor: *clink, scrape, scrape*. Then silence. The steady, rhythmic work had stopped. I listened and peered into the dim light. A hand placed a bucket in the passage and a voice whispered, 'Still, Hey-Ho, keep still.'

Hey-Ho barked again.

'Shh, Hey-Ho!'

I tiptoed closer and saw him, head low and chomping, only the long black-tipped ears poking above the trough, and I smiled at the sweetness of that: one upright, the other lopsided and drooping.

Hey-Ho nosed Captain and brayed again.

'Sssh . . .' Captain whispered. 'Not talk so much.'

He set the shovel down between the lines. I slipped behind the rump of a copper-coloured she-mule, hoping she was not a kicker. Captain was walking towards me, the bucket in his hands. I shrank back against the she-mule. With whip-crack speed, a hind leg lifted, crooked, and a hoof hit my shin. I yelped and doubled over. Captain dropped the bucket and ran. I tried to call out to him, but there was no answer except for the clanking of the bucket as it rolled lonesomely down the aisle. I sank to the ground, just out of reach of the she-mule and I was cursing her for a miserable, mincing, malevolent, malicious, murderous, monstrous molly, and I don't know how long I went on like that but I was sitting there cursing and whimpering when it slowly dawned on me that someone was laughing – just like that: *laughing* – while I whimpered, and the sound of it was sort of tumbling and twinkling, like water running over stone. I looked up, and Captain was standing there, all shiny-eyed with mirth, so I scowled at him. Still laughing, he crouched and lifted my leg and ran his hands over the shinbone; small hands, but assured and competent.

'All right, bone is all right,' he said, pressing the skin just where it was turning the colour of one of Mother's ripest aubergines. 'Father is a doctor,' he added.

'I was looking for you,' I said, still scowling at him. He made as if to stand and I clutched at his arm. He was as light on his feet as a bird, you see, always ready to take flight then; thin, too, as a sparrow.

'Does anyone know – your father, does he know you're here?' I asked. He started a little at that, so I held his arm firmly,

'You can trust me,' I told him. 'I won't say anything to anyone.'

Still ready to fly, he watched me carefully, then said – and his gaze was frank and open as his eyes met mine: 'Father always told me, trust nobody.'

'I won't say anything,' I repeated. 'You see, I'm not supposed to be here either.' I waited an instant, then with my forefinger drew two numbers on the dusty surface of the floor:

15

Captain raised his eyes and a smile opened slowly across his face. He moved his hand to the ground. His forefinger hesitated an instant, then wrote:

14

'Why're you here?' I asked.

Fear and regret flickered across his face but I went on clumsily, 'Are you in the Army too?'

He was suddenly free, and on his feet, and running, silent and barefoot, down the aisle. I stayed there, cursing myself now for asking, because I already knew he wasn't in the army.

PART II

GALLIPOLI

Aboard the *Victoria*

17 August 1915

I dressed carefully that night, following every instruction they'd given us, my fingers shaking a little as I hung my identity disc round my neck. Captain had no such thing, it occurred to me then, and I wondered what he would do when we landed; where he would go. I wondered, too (because I still cared about such things then) if Abel Rudge knew how many rules there were in the Army, that they even told you how to pack your socks: one pair in the pocket of your great coat and one in your kitbag, at the bottom of it.

Gallipoli.

We'd land in the dark of the pre-dawn and surprise the Turk and drive him at point of bayonet back into the hills.

I was blacking the brass buttons of my tunic to stop the glint of them drawing fire when I felt the throb in the belly of the *Victoria*, heard the rumble of her engine and roll of her chain, and grew nauseous with fear.

Gallipoli.

'There'll be little opposition – there aren't many Turks in the immediate area. You'll have no difficulty reaching your objective.'

That was what Colonel Colville had told us.

The *Victoria* fought her way to the mouth of the bay. Every deck rail was thick with men from all the corners of the British world. Ships, ships and more ships, all heading out of the harbour together.

'A gathering,' whispered Firkins, 'to quicken the blood with pride.'

Firkins was still in a rousing, history-in-the-making sort of mood, but my own blood had turned to water.

The crew of a warship gave us a rousing cheer as we rounded the mouth of the bay.

'You fellows can smoke and talk quietly but all lights out when I give the orders,' the Captain said.

The *Victoria* picked up speed. The breeze lifted our hair – we were in the thick of the fleet now, and we were, all of us, racing, bow by bow, to that tail-end of Europe I'd seen from the hill. Navy searchlights swept the sea. Across the water I saw flashing lights, little dots and dashes of Morse.

An old sailor moved along the deck handing round hot cocoa. Firkins was standing beside me, and it occurs to me now that he'd got the shakes too, because he'd stopped talking for once about Jason and the Argonauts and all of that. It might have been the pitch and roll of the open sea that made me vomit, but it was more likely (and I don't like to admit it even now, when nothing matters any more) the sound of the revolving grindstones that really did it. You see, Merrick and Robins were sharpening their bayonets and the glint of the knife edges in the dark made me think that in every nook and cranny of Gallipoli there'd be a bunch of turbaned Turks, and that all the hills glittered with naked, sharpened blades.

'No talking. No light. We're going in now.'

A shiver rippled along the deck. There was silence but for the purr and growl of the engine and the splatter of water against the bow. The air was bitter. We huddled into our greatcoats, each of us alone with his thoughts and fears. The *Victoria* was making for what might have been a beach, set between two headlands, hills rising in a watchful semicircle round a bay. At the mouth of Suvla sat our warships, and there was something about them waiting there in readiness to protect us that made me almost retch again. I'd have given everything, just then, to be back at Bredicot.

I shifted the pack on my back, thinking of all the things that were in there – water bottle, mess tin; shirts – two; socks – eight; handkerchief; pyjamas; towels – two; soap, notebook, pencil, prayer book, two boxes of matches, two hundred rounds, three days' iron rations – thinking, too, as I glanced from the hills to what looked like shingle at their feet, that it might be better, like Captain, to have no pack. I thought of Hey-Ho and the officers' horses and wondered how they'd manage here. Trumpet would've been no good in this country, used as he was to a gentle meadow with a carpet of cowslips and clover.

The moon faded and we glided through that deep, pitchy dark that comes just before dawn.

There'll be little opposition.

The Colonel's words played in my head as we drew closer.

In the dark there were darker shadows, forms that glided to and fro, one of them a troopship, perhaps, by the shape of her, and she was closing in to the shore, launching pontoons, someone said, which together would form a quay. The *Victoria* reached the mouth of the bay. She trembled as her speed slackened. My heart was flapping just then like a windsock, and my limbs shaking, so I held one arm across the other to stop them quivering, and braced myself against the weight of my kit. The *Pasha* was already in the bay and I saw movement down her flank, troops scaling the ladders down into a string of rowing boats.

The *Victoria*'s engines stopped. Messages were exchanged in the dark. The tow that ferried the rowboats from the *Pasha* was close to the shore, behind her the rowing boats, white as Mother's pearls against the dark water.

A destroyer glided up alongside us.

'Proceed to Suvla Bay.'

Not a word was spoken now above a whisper as the *Victoria* sliced through the inky water. Merrick and everyone were looking up at the sky again, wondering how long we had till dawn. I thought of Captain. The mules would be the last to disembark, and Captain would have a rough time of it if it had grown light.

'Remain steady, men, and strict silence.'

Beasley was seeing to the closing of his cartridge pouch. I placed my rifle between my knees and did the same, hoping the dark hid my trembling fingers.

A picket-boat was approaching us. Old Colonel Colville stood, arms folded, at our bow, inspecting the bay, as casual as if he'd got money on a horse and the sea were the green Ludlow turf.

'Closer in! Closer in!' A naval officer stood beckoning from the prow of the picket, behind him twelve rowing boats. When my turn came at the ladder, I breathed deeply to staunch the telltale quivering of my jacket, then jumped the last few feet into the tow.

'Man the boats, men!'

A barge was waiting to draw up alongside the *Victoria*. She was coming for the animals, I thought. The picket turned for the shore and quickened her speed. I heard the lapping of the waves and felt the thump of my heart.

'Go ahead and land!'

'Stay close. Make sure you have the quicker finger,' whispered Beasley to me, grinning and crooking his trigger finger.

The picket was struggling to get closer in to the shore. Beasley shifted in his seat, readying himself, and then we were all shifting, all readying ourselves, all loading magazines. The picket had slipped the rope and was turning back. I saw officers motioning, urging men up the beach. Tandy and Sparrow were trying to disentangle the oars from our legs and kitbags, hoping to row us closer in. It was growing lighter, and the Lieutenant was fidgety and anxious to get ashore. Our string of boats was running into one another, the men in the first boat already scrambling ashore.

I remember what happened next very clearly, because time slowed almost to a standstill, and every second is frozen, as if in a photograph. A single shot rang out. We turned our heads to one another. Suddenly the hill tops spurted red and were laced with running fire.

'Overboard!' the Colonel roared.

There was a great crash and boom. My gut twisted. We turned, as one, from the hill tops to the bay and watched, open-mouthed.

'Good God,' said the Lieutenant.

The Turk howitzers had opened fire on our

transports – they'd got our range – the barge that had drawn up to the *Victoria* – she'd been hit, a great hole ripped in her gut. On her deck there was pandemonium, men running, shouting, screaming. There were two mules – more – five, six perhaps – all stampeding. Somewhere, from a different boat, fragments of 'O God, Our Help in Ages Past' drifted somehow through the roars and crashes. The water of the bay, lashed with a hail of Turk fire, grew white with froth.

'Overboard! Overboard!' roared old Colonel Colville again.

Where was Captain?

There was another ear-splitting crash and the barge was hit again. Captain, Hey-Ho – they'd be there somewhere but I couldn't make anything out, such confusion and chaos and smoke there was. I heard disembodied shouts and screams and suddenly the barge was dipping at her stern.

'Get the animals overboard! Push 'em off! Push them off!'

As the smoke cleared I made out figures on the deck, some scrambling up the deck rail, some hurling themselves over, mules all bunched together. A man was lashing them – not Hey-Ho, the shape was too stout – trying to push one from behind as the barge lurched from side to side. The terrified shrieks of the animals pierced even the deafening roar of fire. One animal stood alone, rigid with fear, legs braced against the tilting deck.

'Come on, Bayliss, get ready,' said Lieutenant Straker.

'All documents destroyed!' the Paymaster was shouting. A wireless man crawled along the deck, a steel chest in his arms.

'Billy, Billy!' It was the Lieutenant and he was pulling me, but I resisted.

Men and animals were jumping from the sides of the barge.

'Water knee-deep below deck!'

I saw Captain – suddenly I saw him – on the near deck – shouting across the water: 'Father! Apa! Father!'

He ran to the far side, searching the deck . . . That was Hey-Ho – head down, careering from port to starboard.

'Make your landing, lads, where you can,' shouted the Colonel, who seemed only the tiniest bit ruffled by what was happening.

Words of warning passed from man to man along my side of the deck, then from Beasley to me.

'There's barbed wire in the water, the current's strong . . .'

I barely heard. *Get him off, get Hey-Ho off*, I was thinking. *Go on. Lash him. Lash him.* I'd do the same, if it were Trumpet and me, I wouldn't leave, not till I'd got Trumpet off.

'All ashore, lickety-spit.' Colville was still barking in a jolly sort of way as if we were all schoolboys on an excursion.

'Father! Apa! Apa!' Captain screamed. I saw him lean out over the handrail waving frantically. He turned to rip a buoy from the splintering deck rail. As the barge settled deeply into the water at her stern he hurled the buoy into the water. *His Father can't swim,* I thought, *neither can Captain.* Hey-Ho shrieked and spun round, shrieked again, and Captain was running after him, dodging and leaping coils of rope and the loose things that slid down the deck.

'Abandon ship!' came a yell from the barge.

Captain scrambled along on all fours; he'd got a rope around Hey-Ho, was dragging him to reach a point from which they could jump overboard. The water around the barge was splattered with fire. A great rending and hissing erupted from her as her rafts and rams splintered to matchwood.

'All ashore!' Colville was still yelling to us in the rowing boats.

The barge suddenly reared into the air, then began to plummet, stern first, the water rushing and roaring at her in a foaming crest, bits of wood shooting out of the quivering water, jagged and splintering things snapping from her deck. Where were Captain and Hey-Ho?

'Chop-chop!' roared the Colonel.

'Overboard, Bayliss, now!' the Lieutenant said, grasping my arm and pushing. 'Just get to that ridge, get to the ridge, then get down.'

A low ridge ran along the curve of that bay and I wondered if it gave any kind of cover. A cheer went up on the beach as our naval guns at last began to roar, men shouting to one another in joy as our guns belched fire, and the peal of them was like nothing I'd ever heard. The enemy guns fell silent, in shock, perhaps at our own, and in their silence I took my chance and threw myself into the water.

I don't remember any more of what happened in the minutes that followed, nor in what order. It might be the fever in me now or it might be that I couldn't apprehend it all at the time, but all I see are flashes of things glimpsed passingly and they are all confused now and muddled in my head. But I can feel the barbed tentacles of wire snag the cloth of my uniform and rip the flesh of my shins, still see the men sorting crates as shrapnel fell in showers round them, still see other men scuttle like rabbits up the beach, still feel the swirl of the current, the slippery shingle, still see the water red with blood.

'Up the beach! Up the beach!'

Somehow or other I reached that small ridge and flung myself down on the sand beside the Lieutenant and Merrick. They were wriggling to get their packs off, both now fixing bayonets. I did the same, conscious of

Lieutenant Straker's deft hands when I was all fingers and thumbs.

'Up to the foot of the hill! Get to the gully!' the Beach Master was shouting through a megaphone.

'Come on,' whispered Lieutenant Straker. He was gentle, and sort of encouraging, and I knew he didn't speak to Beasley or anyone else like that. He and Merrick rose and raced to the base of the hills. Paralysed with fear I clung to the shingle. A moment or two passed like that till I was given a sharp prod. An officer was standing over me, pistol cocked.

'Move on. Join your unit.'

I turned my head to reach for my pack.

'Up the beach, turn left, go uphill three miles and try to find your unit. Now.'

Between the spumes of sand, the spurting water, falling clods and swelling smoke, I glimpsed, just above the dark waterline, a single ear bobbing comically. Hey-Ho's long silvery nose was headed in a calm and purposeful line for the shore, the curve of a slender arm over his neck and on either side a figure almost submerged.

Suvla Bay

18 August 1915, late afternoon

'Up!'

A flattish stretch of coarse grass and scrub and scattered thistle lay ahead.

'Move on, move on!'

By a ruined building at the foot of the cliff, we were assembled into an approximate sort of order, battalions all mixed up, then loaded with provisions and harried on up a rugged, near vertical track.

All that morning we Yeomen were on fatigues. Up and down that barbarous hill we trudged, humping ammunition, kit, rations, firewood, three miles up, three miles down, all in the brutal blast of the sun. There were mules too, laden to the rafters, each picking his way up the loose and slipping stone, but Hey-Ho wasn't among them. In the gully I saw some Australians – big, easy, comfortable men, always laughing and joshing, whatever sort of shape they were in, a group of them coming down as I went up. One looked at me and I was probably looking uncertain or sort of hopeless because he said, 'Watch, out kid. Jacko's everywhere up there.' I must've looked confused because he said, 'Abdul . . . Johnny Turk . . . Jacko. He's all over the place.' I clenched my rifle and he smiled and shook his head in a despairing kind of way, clapped me on the back and went on.

I paused for breath at the elbow of the gully and watched a picket-boat approach the jetty, a string of pinnaces behind her. The officers were still on the beach, still herding men into line. I saw, too, before the foot of the gully, by the ruined building and the stacks of provisions, a donkey grazing in the shrub – Hey-Ho. Captain, too, would be there, if he'd made it. As I was about to turn and race down I was pulled roughly to one side. A Major was shouting, ordering more men aside.

'You – you – you – and you lot there, Into line! Into line!'

Merrick and Tandy and I were rounded up into a makeshift unit.

'You – get reinforcements at the double. You lot – take the goat track branching left off the main gully. Get to the top, get to the hollow, then get to the higher ridge and cover the gully. There're Yeomen up there – unsupported – vulnerable from the far side of the gully. Keep low. Try to make contact with the troops on both sides. Hold the contact – hold the position and dig in.'

I wiped my face on my sleeve, then set off back up a narrow track. It steepened, then disintegrated, and we clawed and gripped the rock to haul ourselves up. At a small plateau we crawled forward in a squirming line. Lieutenant Straker was up there ahead and when we reached him, I paused to rest. He gestured to a small ridge ahead.

'Our men are up there.'

I wiped my streaming face on the shredded cloth of my sleeve. We were motioned onward by some officer or other up ahead.

'Keep low, boyo,' whispered the Lieutenant. I didn't like that he was so familiar with me when he wasn't with the others, him being a Second Lieutenant and me being just a private.

We wriggled like snakes. Fear clawed at my nerves, barbed things tore at my skin, the sun blazed on my back.

Lieutenant Straker froze. After a second or two he inched back.

'Don't move a muscle. We've been seen.'

I glimpsed one – two – three – *three* Turks – snipers – so close – no, *fifteen* or more, and not more than fifty feet away – unearthly and strange as sprites – green-faced and crowned with thorns and twigs. The Australian was right: Jacko was everywhere, in every nook and cranny of the place, and there was nothing but thistles between us and him. I was trembling violently, fingers clawing at the ground. Stealthy and silent, the Lieutenant fixed bayonet. I did the same, fumbling and shaking at it, but when I looked up the Turks were melting away, disappearing like wild cats into the undergrowth.

'Dig in, for God's sake get down and dig in.'

Dig in, to bare rock?

There was a sudden savage shriek somewhere to the right, then the sound of fighting, hand to hand, one man against the other, going at it like wild animals with stones and teeth.

A bullet raced past immediately to my left – I felt the long purring breath of it almost on my skin, long and low – then thudded into a rock at my heels. I was still jittery and shaking as the Lieutenant fired, fired and fired again, and the whole unit was firing, only I'd dropped my rifle, was fumbling with the ammunition and I heard the faint amusement in the Lieutenant's voice. 'Thank you, Bayliss,' as he picked up my fallen round to load his own rifle. You see, I'd not yet fired a shot.

A bullet smacked into the spine of a rock inches to my left and ricocheted off. Suddenly there was yelling all around.

'Turk advancing!'

Immediately ahead a line of Turks was rising shoulder to shoulder, steel flashing, too many of them to say, and we were only ten men.

Disembodied voices yelled from the rocks and ridges, regular soldiers taking the command.

'Back! Get back!'

The Lieutenant hesitated, looked quickly to the rear, then hissed, 'Straight to the gully when I say – not the path, but to the right . . . Quick now, run!'

Bent low, we raced, scrambling back, slipping and stumbling. Merrick and Tandy were somewhere to my left, I think, when I hurled myself over the brim of that gully. I glimpsed for a split second, too late, a vertical drop – and fell, dropping my rifle, flailing, tumbling, falling, grasping at a sapling, losing it, clasping at another, falling faster, then caught up and tangled and held briefly in some wretched thorny thing, the stones rolling and crashing beneath, dirt in my eyes, grit in my teeth and ears and nose. And if Jacko ever saw me there quivering in mid-air and all tangled in that pitiful tree with no rifle and never even having fired a shot, he must've been laughing even harder than Merrick and all the others would have.

The tree bent and screeched, the roots of it torn from the rock, and I fell again.

Some time passed before I came to. I felt water on my lips and tilted my head to drink. I was lifted and wrapped as if in the velvety black of the sky and carried away.

Sometime later, when I woke again, not knowing if it were the same night, there was pitchy blackness directly over me but if I lifted my head I could see the water of the bay glimmering there, the flickering lights and shadows moving across the white shingle, mules and men, collecting and delivering, loading and unloading, sorting and arranging. Above them all the stars swayed and swung and were both brighter and lower than any I'd ever seen. I was a little concussed still, perhaps, but I saw now that the blackness above me was only the shadow of the cliff.

A medic was moving there, along the base of the cliff, from man to man. I called out for water but he did not come. Amidst the shrubby things that stood in silvery outline against the black of the cliff sat a figure, and it was he who turned his head in answer when I called.

He smiled, then bent over his work once more, his arm moving in and out and up and down, in and out and up and down: Captain – his head bowed, raising his arm to pull, lowering it to push.

My head throbbed and my lids were leaden and dropping, but I heard a donkey bray and when my lids closed, the movement of Captain's arm still played behind them: pulling up and pushing down. I saw a rose-coloured quilt, Mother's day room, her tapestry chair, her right hand, with the slim gold band, pushing a needle in, pulling it out.

Sewing. Captain was sewing, sewing and crying as he stitched a corporal's stripes back on to a sleeve.

His Father's sleeve. Captain had kept the stripes and now he was sewing them on to his Father's uniform. I opened my eyes and saw him pat and smooth his work, and though I am a plain country boy it seemed to me then that the stars were there that night only to light his work and to silver the tears on his cheeks.

He bent over his father's head and kissed it.

Later, when I woke again, there was the light of a match moving at my side. Captain had what looked like a strip of packing crate in his hands and he was holding the flame of the match closely to the wood. Captain saw me turn to watch, held a hand to my forehead, asked how I felt.

'OK.' I said – a little tersely – because I was worried he might've seen me looking foolish in the branches of that thorn tree.

'Good,' he said, with his slow smile. 'Good.'

He bent his head again to the work he was at, then picked up another longer strip of packing crate and bound it with string at right angles two-thirds up the other. A packing crate cross with a name burned on it.

'I am sorry,' I said.

He touched his forehead to the tip of the cross and sat for a good while like that. When he looked up I asked, 'Why did you come here?'

He answered with the same openness with which he'd spoken in Alexandria, the same seriousness, but his tone was matter-of-fact and there was no self-pity in it.

'I did not like to see Father work so hard.' He put a hand to his own chest. 'Bad heart. After – after we lost our home – over the mountains, so far, with Hey-Ho, all our things on top –' he gestured to Hey-Ho's back – 'then Mother, when she got ill, we left the things – Hey-Ho carried Mother . . . maybe two hundred miles . . .' He looked away.

After a while – and now his eyes were glimmering with guilt and anger – he said, 'I took extra grain for Hey-Ho – in Alexandria – because he is tired. Every day, only a little . . .' His eyes blazed. 'The Major—'

'I know,' I said. 'I know.'

He bent his forehead to the cross again.

'I saw,' I said. 'I saw – you and Hey-Ho, you saved him in the water.'

'It was his heart,' he said. 'We saved him from the water but we could not save his heart.' He gestured to the ruined building at the northern end of the bay. 'I covered him with stones. There is no earth here . . . only stones.'

A long time passed then, I think, before he said, 'Hey-Ho carried you, too . . . you fell maybe twenty feet.' Then he lifted his head and told me I'd fallen, that it had been a while till he'd found me, that Hey-Ho had carried me down the gully.

I held out a hand to Hey-Ho, calling him.

Hey-Ho brayed in answer but did not move.

'Very loud donkey,' said Captain, a faint smile broaching his grave face. 'Come, Hey-Ho, come quietly.'

Hey-Ho stepped gingerly towards us.

Captain rose, the packing crate cross in one hand, the other on Hey-Ho's droppy ear.

'Father . . . said . . . "Look after Hey-Ho." Last thing he said . . . "Look after Hey-Ho" . . .'

Sometime later that night he returned without the cross. We talked for a long time then. There were tears and there were long silences, and he was simple and unreserved when he did talk but he never spoke of his father again that night. It was too soon, just then.

Suvla Bay

19 August 1915

I woke again as glimmers of dawn lit the water. In the last minutes before sunrise, mules and carts hurried across the beach, men dragged up field guns and ammunition, other men built jetties.

At sunrise the water was lashed with a hail of enemy bullets. The men on the beach paused, then continued their unloading. From the safe lee of the cliff I picked out Captain and Hey-Ho there at the jetty, Hey-Ho still and patient as Captain fixed water-cans to him and they went about their work, to and fro, while shells crashed and ploughed into the shingle, stirring the water to a white froth. I listened to the buzzing of the flies and the delirious babbling of the wounded that lay in a row to my left. They brought me food, but I couldn't eat the bread or the biscuit and saved them for Hey-Ho. His digestive system must be stronger than mine if he could eat the biscuit they gave us there.

*

When the sun was at its height, the beach was still thick with men. The day wore on. The water glittered in the dropping sun, the boats all dipping sweetly it.

Night came again. My head had cleared. Tentatively I moved my bruised limbs. The green lights of the hospital ship were strung like a necklace along her side, a great red cross in her centre. There'd be white sheets and blankets there, but I wasn't a case for a hospital ship, hadn't been hit, hadn't even fired a shot. That hospital ship might've taken me home to Mother, to Francis, Geordie and Liza but I'd have had to tell them how I'd been scared even before we sailed, that my sleep was haunted by bodies stacked any old way, one on top of the other, the dead alongside the living, on an Egyptian dock, that I hadn't wanted to drink in the Egyptian bars, or sing as I stepped off the boat at Gallipoli, that I still hadn't fired a single shot.

Lieutenant Straker found me there under the cliff and had a word with the doctor. I was still wary of the Lieutenant but I saw now he had a kindness in him, enough not to notice my fear, enough to ask the doctor to give me another night, to say for the minute I wasn't needed.

Chocolate Hill

21 August 1915

'Bayliss. We attack this afternoon. Rejoin the unit. Collect entrenching tools. Abandon pack and greatcoat. At the crook of the gully, take the left fork and keep going.' The line of the Lieutenant's jaw was tense and hard and I thought better of telling him that my head was still aching. Captain and Hey-Ho and I were standing side by side. I turned to Captain and whispered, 'What will you do?'

'Bayliss,' the Lieutenant snapped. 'Go on up straight away.'

'You – and the donkey! You – boy!' Chips shouted. 'Over here!'

That was the first time I saw Chips. At the mouth of the gully that ran up from the centre of the bay, a mountain of provisions beside him, a largish man sat hunched beside the water-cans, the hump of his back intended to signal his disgust at the height of the hill someone had in mind for him to climb and the disconcerting absence of buses or hansom cabs.

Chips was with the Catering Corps, but assigned to our unit. He was a man not given to motion of any kind. He was appalled, you see, coming as he did from flat country around the Thames Estuary, at the crags and gullies of Gallipoli. He'd seen Hey-Ho and his eyes had brightened at the sight of a donkey, unladen and without any obvious occupation.

'Who is he, Bayliss?' the Lieutenant asked me, pointing to Captain.

'Sir, Captain, sir.'

Captain saluted, answering the Lieutenant's question to me with surprising confidence and dignity. The harsh lines of the Lieutenant's face relaxed into a smile.

'Captain, is it? Well, Chips here has his eye on that animal of yours. We'll see if you and that donkey can live up to your name, shall we?'

And so it was that I was sent back up the hill, that Captain was absorbed into the Yeomanry, and little Hey-Ho was loaded with clanking cans filled with water from Alexandria.

We parted, Captain and I, with a smile.

'See you,' he said.

'So long,' I said. 'Don't forget me. It's thirsty work up there.'

He smiled again, and I knew he could see even then that I was scared.

It was mighty long and steep, that gully, and there were sections of it that had signs like:

DUCK AND RUN!

That was mostly in the crooks and doglegs of the gully that were open to enemy fire, and you went past them at a run with your heart flapping like a loose sail against your ribs.

The trenches wound up and down and all along the hillside. There were hundreds of corners and kinks and elbows and long, straight traverse sections. In one of those traverses I found Tandy and Robins and Firkins and the others. Tandy asked to borrow my field glasses.

'Look, Billy.' He handed them back to me. 'Chocolate Hill, the lowish one, brown-coloured,' he whispered. 'Then look due east from the Salt Lake and you can see it. That's the one we're going to take. We've got men up there, Billy, in dugouts under cover of the hill.' I clenched the muscles of my legs to stop them shaking, wondering if Tandy had seen, but he was still watching the ridge.

'How will it feel?' I asked. 'Killing a man?'

'It's him or you, Billy, him or you.' He smiled gently, 'You have no choice.' He smiled again, 'See, they're below, just below the knoll.'

The ridge ran from one high point at one end of

the bay to the other. The lower slopes blazed yellow with gorse, the tops straggled with Scots pines. I picked out scattered infantry, all as dusty-coloured as the trees and scrub.

'Just beyond Chocolate Hill is Scimitar Hill and beyond that to the North is "W" Hill. They're held by the Turks, there are guns on the tops of them.' I picked out the Turkish infantry too in the low scrub in the front of the hill, beyond it the bulges and buttresses of Sari Bair.

We waited in line. I fingered my Lee-Enfield. Would I fire this time? If it was him or me, would I kill? The Lieutenant crawled up, behind him a handful or so of men.

'Go over, boys.'

Go over? When the slightest flicker of a thistle would draw fire? If I moved so much as a finger I'd be riddled with bullets, killed thousands of times over. The enemy was behind every bristle, every stone and rock of this place. My fingers tightened around the gun. This time I would not drop it, this time I would fire. I must have the quicker finger, Beasley had said. It's him or me. Him or me.

We moved off, hands and noses in the dusty scree, crawling up beneath rocky ribs and knolls and strange outcrops, protected only by a minute rise in the land.

'All right, stop here, boys. Dig in and hold on till the artillery come.'

Isolated fragments of us, all different battalions and units, settled into every cranny and depression alongside and to the rear. Again there was a long wait.

In the early afternoon our battleships came in close to the bay and began to bombard the enemy positions on the two hills. The first shell fell with a sobbing shriek and hurtled deep into the earth, hurling stones and dust up, engulfing the enemy line in clouds of white smoke. The earth beneath me trembled with the impact. The cannons roared and shells screamed over our heads, the air whimpered and moaned, and the roaring breath of the shells was on my face. Every battleship and cruiser and field gun and howitzer was firing, and the din of them seemed to force its way into the gap between my brain and the bone of my skull.

After an hour the bombardment stopped, there was a second's silence, then the instruction, 'Forward!'

The line rose and walked forward as if on a parade ground. I was still standing, undone with fear, made senseless by the din of it all, my brain turned liquid, my legs watery. The Lieutenant turned and yelled, 'One foot in front of the other, Bayliss, just one foot in front of the other.'

Everything inside me turned pulpy and quivering. I couldn't think, couldn't move, you see, in all the din of machine guns, artillery, bombs, rifles and all the battleships in the bay firing broadsides.

'Fire!'

They were, all of them, just walking, steady and straight, into an inferno, an inferno of all kinds of explosive and shrapnel.

One foot in front of the other, Billy, just one foot in front of the other.

I was walking and it seemed extraordinary how much shrapnel there could be, how I could feel the tear and whisper of it on my skin and still not be hit.

One foot in front of the other, just one foot in front of the other.

Bullets screamed into stones. The field guns roared, machine guns rattled, rifles cracked and snapped. Old Colonel Colville stumbled. Our line never wavered. I did as the others did, I never flinched or turned my head. Lying on the ground, the gallant old man waved us on.

'Forward, boys, forward!' were his last words.

The line moved on and I went too, one foot after another, just one foot after another. My rifle was levelled then, and there was something about Colville lying there on the stone, the crimson stain on his tunic, perhaps because he waved us on so cheerily, perhaps because he'd have known Father, but after I saw him there, left to die in the blazing sun, I fired that rifle. I fired. Fired and fired and fired till it burned to the touch and I couldn't see for the tears in my eyes.

Apperley fell, and Cooper, and great holes opened up in our ranks . . . Tandy went down too, and there were men falling all around.

I reached a place, somehow or other I got there – it must've been an old Turk trench – quite deep – and we paused to regroup – a minute or two only – and went on – men in the ranks taking command. One foot in front of the other, one foot in front of the other, into the range of a thousand rifles, into murderous, intense fire.

I don't remember when exactly but at some point the scrub on the right caught fire and the blaze spread across the dry and crackling ground. The flames crept up on the wounded and the fallen. We moved on, and never turned our heads, leaving them to shrivel in the sun and the flames but I can still hear now the screams of them, screams that pierced even the shriek of the guns.

That day was a slaughter.

Dark fell like dust over the hill and the spurts of red from the enemy died down. The ground was soaked in the blood of the Yeomen. Contorted bodies lay thick as pile everywhere, faces half shot away, some killed even before they fired a shot, mostly Yeomanry farmers in the pink and prime of life. I don't like to look back into that day, into the din and flames and horror of it . . . No, there was never anything like it again.

By night fires had broken out all over – the ridges were blazing too, the flames leaping and spreading into one another, bathing the slopes in blood-red light. The moans and cries of the wounded rose to the stars. Here and there an arm rose, begging for water. Some of those left out there scraped their way back.

Somehow, the end of the day had come, and I was still there.

Officers crept along the line trying to consolidate our position, to get us into some sort of order.

'Dig in, or they'll have their shrapnel on you at dawn.'

The Fusiliers came up to help bring in the wounded and that was terrible work – blind or without their reason or unrecognizable the wounded mostly were. But the stretcher-bearers and the Fusiliers went about up there as orderly as if in some green-gold corner of England.

I stared, struck dumb by the day, into the night. The Colonel. Apperley, Cooper, Tandy . . . I sat there among the sandbags, the ammunition, the bodies, among all the debris of battle, while the cold white searchlights of the destroyer raked back and forth over the burning hills.

Captain was as good as his word. He came up with the mule train, asked for the Yeomen and was directed to us. He was wearing an approximate sort of uniform, a rifle slung over his shoulder, water-cans stacked either side of Hey-Ho, who was grazing in the scrub, his legs hobbled so he couldn't stray beyond the slight rise that sheltered him from the enemy guns.

'Billy? Billy?'

Slowly I raised my head.

'How are you?'

I drank down the can of water he handed me.

'Were you scared?'

'The waiting was the worst,' I answered, not telling all the truth, not telling I'd not gone forward with the others, that the Lieutenant had yelled at me, that I'd gone like a child, one foot in front of the other, and that as I went one single feeling had filled my head: that if I kept going, if I went on and on, I'd suddenly reach green fields, see a church spire, a half-timbered house . . .

I didn't tell him any of that. Instead I looked at him and said, 'When they're right up close, and the air is thick with them, the bullets sort of purr and whistle in your ears.' Captain looked at me quizzically. I rushed on, gaining steam. 'But I don't mind that. And the shrapnel, it's like a whoosh, like a crashing gust of wind . . .'

'I know, Billy. I know shrapnel, I know bullets,' said Captain. 'I have heard them. Only in Egypt were we safe. When we got to Egypt it was safe . . .'

I bowed my head. It was a fair and gentle rebuke. When all I'd known in life was cricket and croquet and tea in the nursery at Bredicot, Captain had been driven out of his home, had crossed mountains on foot.

He had something in his hands, I noticed then – something rifle-shaped and wrapped in a blanket. He handed it to me, holding out his own hand for my rifle in exchange.

'For tomorrow,' he said, and I saw from the shine in his eyes that he was proud. I unwrapped it. The gun had bits of wood and glass and wire rigged in a box over it – a periscope – a periscope made to fit a rifle. I put my eye to it. With it I could see everything without exposing my head. I turned to him in amazement but Captain's face was serious.

'I am scared for you,' he said simply. 'I'll come up with the relief. When it comes up, I will be here again.'

He went to Hey-Ho. The little donkey picked his way on those butterfly legs of his, back over the rock and thistle, between the bodies and all the wreckage of war, the shards of wood and metal. Hands beckoned at every step, men crying out for water. They stopped, gave water, and moved on. When they had no more to give, I saw Captain stoop and help a wounded man on to that little donkey's back then turn and head for the gully.

There weren't enough mules at Gallipoli, you see, to carry the water; there were never enough mules and never enough water. I don't think the Generals had measured those hills before they sent us over there; they'd not thought about how we'd get things up and down, and those stout and plucky pack-animals went up and down, up and down the gullies, and we, up there in the blazing sun, depended on them for our lives.

It was bitterly cold, too cold to sleep. Men twitched and started in their sleep. Others moaned and whimpered like dogs. Firkins was close to losing his reason that night. It might have been because he lost his pipe that he dug a deeper hole for himself than anyone, and was scratching and clawing at the ground like a terrier.

They came up once more that night with water, Captain and Hey-Ho, and went back and forth among the wounded. As they went to and fro under the stars, I watched them and I saw how very unlike a donkey was to a horse. I began to think that even Trumpet could be improved by little bits of Hey-Ho: his patience, perhaps, and the delicacy of his hoofs. Hey-Ho had the mournful ancient eyes of all his species, but he was in some ways more donkey than any other. His cans clanked more merrily than those of any other, his bray was louder than any other, his ears somehow sweeter and sadder than any other. He was the quintessence of donkey, all the donkeys of all the centuries distilled in that one little Hey-Ho.

*

Dawn fingered her way over the ridge and met a scene of cruel desolation.

I took position in a ragged line only one man deep; not a line really, just a series of holes of all shapes and sizes. It was the men in the ranks who took command that day. No relief came up. The sun crept higher and still we waited, cowering, still we prayed for reinforcements, for water, for ammunition.

As the sun reached her height, the enemy guns erupted in a great blaze of fire and the guns of our warships answered and swept back and forth with deafening thunder. We waited in the sweltering heat, still praying for reinforcements, for water and ammunition. There was no information, no orders, nothing. The enemy fire died down, the enemy line seeming to melt and fade towards the knoll.

In the middle of the day a unit of Dorsets – fifty or so of them, seventy yards ahead and to the right of us, rose. Immediately they came under fire and we watched in horror as they began to fall. They were pulling back – the line breaking – Jacko was on the move and suddenly his fire was on us and it was coming from right and left and ahead – and we were firing back. I had my periscope, and that was a great help – and there was no hesitation in my using the rifle that day.

Bullets cracked like whips against stone. His gunners had our range, their fire deadly and determined. The air fluttered and moaned in the wake of the shells, and echoed with confusion and screams but we stayed and held our ground – that day at least. We'd no chance – the ground between us just then was the size of a croquet pitch and Jacko had more men, more guns, more ammunition.

After a while his shells came at briefer and briefer intervals.

Again, the day was over and I was still there. There's always that surprise after a battle to find yourself still alive.

That day I'd seen a man fall as I fired, actually seen him fall at a bullet I'd fired. Before then, I'd never been able to tell, there'd always been so much smoke and confusion. It is a big moment in a man's life – in a boy's life – when you first see a man you've hit buckle and bend.

We answered to our names in the dark. For every gap that had opened in our ranks there was silence in answer. Archie Spade was gone, Harry Beasley wounded . . . so many.

'Those that can walk. Those that can stand, into line.'

The command was repeated, with whispered disbelief, mouth to mouth. There'd been no reinforcements: did they not know we were so few? It scarcely seemed credible they would keep us up there, much less send us into a night-time attack. Men half dead were hauling themselves up and crawling to the top of that gully.

'Advance.'

We scrambled out of the gully and into the white glare of the moon.

'Halt. Open fire.'

My hands trembled as I fired. It was exhaustion then, not fear, that made them tremble. The snapping of our bullets swelled to a din. The hill echoed with the screams of the Turkish shells and the rattle of our guns.

Men fell back, dead or wounded, into the gully. I stood senseless with the horror of seeing them bend and break, bodies torn apart.

'Billy, get down!'

It was Captain. He pushed me and I fell, senseless and quivering back into the shallow gully. I heard screams.

'They're coming!'

The Lieutenant was shouting for ammunition, for relief, yelling that Jacko was almost on us. I saw the line of Turks running at us. Captain handed the Lieutenant ammunition. Captain unhooked his own rifle, loaded it and fired, round after round, steely and deadly and accurate.

'Good God,' said Lieutenant Straker, turning to Captain for a brief second. They held off the Turks that were coming at us for a while, Captain and the Lieutenant, but when another wave of them came up, the Lieutenant yelled.

'Get back! Get back!'

Later, that night, further back, in some other line, as Captain turned to leave, the Lieutenant took him by the hand and said, smiling, 'Strictly speaking, the Mule Corps and such like are not allowed to fight.'

In the morning those of us that remained were prodded with the butt of a rifle. We stood to arms in the dim dawn. When it was fully light we stood down to make tea, a filthy, unshaven, hungry-looking man every three yards, huddled over a dirty tin and a meagre fire. Captain came up at six. The well, you see, was at the bottom of the hill. The mules would fetch the water from there, cross the Salt Lake with it and come up at six in the morning and six in the evening. It was a long and dangerous journey and up at the top our water was measured out in thimbles. By that morning – our third up there – a line of dead mules marked the path across the Lake, from start to finish. Jacko kept his eyes on that lake, day and night, not liking to see those animals bringing us up ammunition or water but I never saw that little donkey flinch under any kind of fire. Nor did I see him ever shirk a duty or baulk at any burden.

You had a pal to make tea with or cook bacon with, and up at Chocolate Hill I had to muck in with

Firkins and his new pipe. That morning he didn't talk about the fall of Troy or anything else. I looked at that pipe but didn't like to ask where it came from.

We set to improving our dugouts – we were so close to the enemy, and so close too to the top of the hill we wanted to take. It was within our reach if they'd only given us more men.

'For God's sake, when will they bring up ammunition?' I heard the Lieutenant ask, more of himself than anyone else.

At around seven a.m. there was a sudden burst of heavy fire from the enemy.

By eight the enemy had a new gun in position and the remains of us there were blasted with shrapnel.

'Get back, get back!' Straker yelled.

'The order is to retire!'

Within minutes our trench was taken.

'Retire, all men!'

'Dear God, there *are* no men . . .' Straker whispered.

We crawled away on our bellies like worms. At the cliff edge our tattered company converged with other men, a mass of leaderless men, all drifting down the gully. We stumbled on between the fallen bodies of the wounded and the dead. At a twist in the gully we ran into a Casualty Clearing Station, the wounded, in their hundreds, on the ground, hit again, as they lay there, by enemy guns.

We joined the remnants of the unit and we stood,

those of us that could, for the Major to take the roll-call.

'Allgood . . . Apperley . . . Arrowsmith . . .'

The Major looked up, questioning, paused.

'Bayliss,' he continued.

'Sir.'

'Barnet . . . Beasley . . .'

'Sir.' He had an ugly wound, Beasley, but it was only a flesh wound to the arm.

'Bird . . . Bristow . . . Caradine . . .'

'Sir.'

'Cooper . . . Creswell . . . Deakin . . . Dipple, John . . . Dipple, James . . .'

Our heads bowed. Two days ago the Yeomen had gone into battle a thousand strong, gone over cheering and shouting, the blood hot in their veins. Now scarcely a man remained. Only three hundred answered to their names.

We knew already that we'd had our chance at Gallipoli and missed it. We'd never had the numbers we needed, never had the support we needed. The men who'd died had given all, for nothing, the bit of hill we'd taken lost as the Turks spread out and moved like running water down the slope, killing any man that hadn't run. Now the dead and wounded lay, in their thousands, in lines that stretched from the jetty to the foot of the hills.

There were too many to bury and no earth to bury

them in. Lighters came in to the hospital ship, one after another, night after night. Night after night, the Chaplain stood on the deck, in surplice and cassock, and read the burial service by a single flickering candle, hundreds of us massed on the shoreline, watching in silence. Still figures, wrapped in weighted sailcloth, were placed on the gangplank three at a time, the board lifted, a muted splash, as they slipped, feet first into the silent sea.

There was a general issue of wool, soaked in scent, to muffle the stench of the rotting dead. Those of us that survived were racked with illness, gaunt and sunken-eyed.

Firkins was subdued for a long time. It was a good while before he began to talk again about the heroes of days gone by. His new pipe was a great consolation to him, even though it was a dead man's.

Captain, hoping to lift my black mood, brought me a tin of condensed milk and a notice cut from *The Times*.

'Billy, listen,' he said.

The advance of the English Yeomen 'was a sight calculated to send a thrill of pride through anyone with a drop of English blood running in their veins'. It said too that we were the 'most stalwart soldiers England has ever sent from her shores', that we'd moved up that hill 'like men marching on parade'. The worst of it all, for the loss and the death, was at

Chocolate Hill, and I don't think in all the history of the Worcestershire Yeomen there was ever a day like it.

Those three days up there marked the end of my boyhood because you can't see those things and not be changed. You can't kill a man and not be changed.

Green Hill

Early September 1915

Those of us that could still stand, many with greater wounds than mine, were returned to the ranks to fight. We fought well and proudly and even Johnny Turk wished he'd been on our side and not with Jerry. He was a good and fair fighter and so were we. The Generals on both sides spent our lives like water, but there were never enough of us on our side to hold the bit of ground we'd won.

I was up there on the hill one day, I remember, six o'clock had come and gone and Captain hadn't come up. I watched the beach and thought of the gully and the crook in it, where it was steep and slithery and tricky to hurry a heavily laden donkey, but the Turkish guns were on you there and you had to hurry. Every centimetre of that crook was under constant fire and your life was in your hands at every minute there.

I lifted my field glasses. On the beach men were working half naked, covering carts with bushes to camouflage them. Despite the fire, you see, everything went on – the men stacking ammunition carts, the mules going to and fro. There! That was Captain on his way to the jetty, threading between the carts and the mules and the men who sat there trying to patch or wash their clothes. He nodded in answer to their greetings. Captain and Hey-Ho were now loved by us all. Hey-Ho stood patient, head low, accepting his load. They turned to cross the Salt Lake and pick their way up the gully.

Sometimes the Lieutenant sent me off to guard the train of donkey supplies up the hill and then Captain and I would climb together, tripping and sweating and falling, but that day, as I remember, I'd been kept back on a wiring fatigue.

When the mail had arrived that morning there'd been a great shouting and yelling and hurrahing and men rushing along the trenches, and in all the excitement and row it was impossible to hear the Sergeant yelling out the names. I'd been glad Captain wasn't there. I didn't like him to be there when we got our mail, him having no one to send him anything. A Sergeant-Major had gone along the line, throwing each of us a parcel. There were socks and vests and paper and pencils from the Girl Guides, and I'd taken one extra for Captain. There'd been a parcel from home, too, for me. In it were two jerseys and I smiled to see them because on one of them the stitching was loose and bobbly with lots of loops and holes. Mother had pinned a piece of paper to it: 'Knitted by Liza!' She'd added two pairs of socks, with another label, 'Knitted by your Mother!', and the stitching in those was perfect, though I thought it was odd because one pair was bigger than the other, and when I looked, one jersey was bigger than the other, too. Perhaps they didn't know what size I was now and they'd sent different ones to be sure one would fit. Anyway, I gave the smaller socks and the smaller jersey to Captain and never stopped to think how Liza and Mother knew I'd be in need of socks and warm things.

Firkins had socks too, from his Aunt Alice. They were wrapped in an old copy of the *Malvern Gazette* and I picked that up because it had a picture of the county cricket on the front. We didn't get any newspapers at Gallipoli so they posted news in the form of telegrams on the notice board at the foot of HQ gully. There'd always be a crowd around that board, but I never stopped to read it, the telegrams being mainly about how the Germans were having a bad time of it and other snippets meant to encourage us.

I'd never have read the *Gazette* back at home but that afternoon, as I waited up there, I read everything in it – the weather report, about the harvest and the hay, the stock sales, the carriages for hire, the advertisements for the Kodak cameras that cost thirty-two shillings and sixpence, the announcements, the births and the deaths, and the new window for the cathedral, the donations of woollens to the hospitals. Then I turned back to the page with the cricket and stared at that picture till I was far, far away, lost in the haze and humming and fresh-cut grass of an English summer, and tears were pouring down my cheeks. I didn't notice Captain was there till he took the *Gazette* from my lap. He studied the picture carefully.

'Like this?' he asked. 'Your house?'

It wasn't the cricket that caught his eye, it was the row of houses behind the cricketers, along the far edge of a village green. They were of red brick and stone, and I nodded.

'Yes, more or less.'

He looked at the picture again. Fresh tears welled in my eyes at the thought of Bredicot, but I was dunder-headed and didn't stop to think why Captain might be so interested in houses.

'Look.' He put a tin of condensed milk in my hand. You had to pay a fortune for it on the beach and I was always dreaming of it.

'My house,' said Captain. 'Father said it was made of stone.'

Captain had no one to send him mail, no home that he could remember.

'Your father?' he asked. He'd asked me before but he liked to hear things again, to be told more.

'A doctor, like yours,' I said.

He smiled.

'Both doctors.'

'And a soldier,' I said.

Again he smiled.

'Both doctors and soldiers.'

Perhaps it was because we'd both lost our fathers that we drew so close to each other. Sometimes we'd talk, in the way boys do, men do, reluctantly and briefly, of the things that matter most, but that afternoon he just asked, 'Cows?'

I nodded. 'And Trumpet.'

He nodded, too. 'Your horse. Two brothers?'

'Yes, and Liza.'

'So many,' he said.

The days were now monotonous: long and slow and quiet. All hunger and heat, sweat, stench, flies, filth, dirt and digging. You'd be woken by the sentry at four, stand to arms, then stand down when it was fully light. Then you'd be sent off on a wiring party or some or other fatigue like digging. We were always digging up there and now my trench was good and deep, perhaps ten foot. All along the bottom of its winding course, we had dugouts now to lie and rest in, other dugouts for food and ammunition. We had roofs, too, and sandbag parapets, and blankets to pin up against the sun. We spent long hours in there together, Captain and I, when things were quiet, and I remember how he used to howl with laughter when the walls collapsed and showered us with torrents of earth and stone. They were prone to do that, you see, at any sudden noise or movement.

It was a week later, I think, that I was up there in the late afternoon in a new dugout, composing a letter to Liza, my feet in the sun, back in the shade of the new rug canopy, the shimmering turquoise sea and all its tiny ships laid out below like a painting. It would be an hour or two still before Captain came up, and I listened idly to the *crack-crack-crack* of distant rifle fire and was thinking of how Captain loved the sun and the heat, of his horror of the cold, his deep dislike of winter. He basked like a lizard in the sun, played like a puppy in the sea; when we'd wash in the delicious water of the bay, laughing and ducking, as all of us did when the shrapnel rained around us, he was at his happiest. Jacko didn't like to see us swimming and having fun in his bay at all and loved to pepper the water with his bullets if he saw us in it trying to get clean, but we none of us took much notice, the bay being so big and the Turkish guns being so inaccurate and difficult to aim at that distance. Hey-Ho liked the sea too and, like us, luxuriated in the feeling of being cool and clean, and he'd swim in circles round us, one ear bobbing comically, the other, droppy one floating flat on the surface of the sea.

Things had been quiet in our part of the line that day, and for a while now. Listless shots came over, the bullets droning overhead, landing perhaps with a dull thud in a sandbag. Our rifles would snap back and Jacko would stop, then he'd start up and the whole thing would begin again. With my left hand I counted out, only idly and approximately, the minutes between spurts of rifle fire.

The grass and flowers had been beaten by thousands of steps into a scarred wasteland, no man's land thick with rusting wire and the staring eyes of the unburied dead. A honeycomb of tunnels had spread along the ridge. We had a listening post now, and the engineers had terraced the ground so that reserves could gather in line behind us. Best of all, there were tunnels all the way up to the trench, wide enough for Hey-Ho to pass along, though Hey-Ho mistrusted trenches, devoid as they were of thistle and open sky.

I continued with my letter to Liza. A shell wailed somewhere below. It fell and mushroomed on the beach in a cloud and a fire-burst of falling fragments. For a while the dust stayed suspended until I saw, through it, figures setting back to their work and everything going on as before.

I finished my letter and began to think about the two eggs. That day was once-a-month-egg-day and I could indulge in the luxury of dreaming about what to do with two eggs. I was heartily sick of dried apricots and figs, and longed for bread and jam. The rations were monotonous and dull – tea, sugar and bacon, tinned milk, bread, cheese, potatoes, onions every second day. We still had to have a pal to muck in with, cook with and share all we possessed with, and the Lieutenant didn't seem to mind Captain staying round with me. You see, up there, we drew our rations raw and cooked them in the evenings. One of us would fetch the rations and the other get on with the cooking. It was good to be with someone my own age when Captain came up, and not with a fuddy-duddy like Firkins with his pipe and all the Trojans around him at all hours. At night, when the moon silvered the ridges of the trenches and parapets, we'd sit and cook and talk.

I think mainly because I'd written to Liza, and Liza had a great love of them, I settled in the end on pancakes.

Chips had a short, shallow trench in the stretch next to my dugout, and when I sealed my letter, I looked up and saw him turn his head to the tunnel. Little fires were being lit all up and down the gullies and trenches, and it was time, he was thinking, for Hey-Ho to come up.

There! Chips and I turned to the sacking door to Chips's trench: Hey-Ho's white muzzle was nosing the sacking aside, his long head, dark eyes and now his ears visible. He squeezed carefully through the opening, laden as he was with clanking cans for Chips.

Captain unloaded Hey-Ho, then the little donkey

was free to make his way alone along the trench collecting rewards. There was something about both Captain and Hey-Ho that made men want to do things for them, even if they hadn't risked their lives to reach us each day, so we all saved our biscuit for Hey-Ho. You needed the jaws of a camel to eat the biscuit we were given, but it probably tasted good after thistle, and Hey-Ho didn't make a fuss. Captain saw more provisions than any of us, ferrying them to and fro as he did all day, but he'd smile gratefully when we saved biscuit for Hey-Ho.

I uncurled my fingers, one by one, and held up my hands, keeping one thumb clenched. Captain smiled again and nodded. Nine was good. Nine was the longest, the most minutes that had passed between bouts of fire.

I put our pot on the fire. Chips had two kerosene stoves in his trench, over one a pot for tea, one for lunchtime stew if he was making it. Captain crouched down and took up a stick and prodded our can of water, to keep it upright.

'In my way again,' grumbled Chips.

I cracked the eggs into a billycan and mixed up a batter, then half-inched Chips's frying pan. We grinned and took no notice of his grumbling, it being part of the fun for him, having something other than the Turks to be annoyed about. Chips mumbled a lot to himself and his jaws were always moving, but he rarely spoke more than three or four words at a time out loud if he could help it, and if he did, the words came alongside noisy chewing and swallowing sounds.

Hey-Ho was a dainty animal to have in a trench, never tripping over the legs of sleeping men or knocking over the cans of tea that had taken hours to boil. In any case, he'd wandered away, most probably in the hope of more donations of Army biscuit, so Captain left to fetch him.

'Seen a bit of life . . .' said Chips, folding his arms.

I wasn't sure if he was talking about Hey-Ho or Captain.

'Handy with a rifle too . . .'

Chips plumped his voluminous self down on a sandbag. It was lucky, really, that we didn't rely entirely on Chips for our meals for he showed as little enthusiasm in that direction as he did for any other kind of work. I put some fat in the pan, poured some batter into it, swilling it around the way Liza did to cover the base of the pan. Chips looked on sceptically. I flipped the pancake, rather well I thought.

'Waste of good eggs . . .'

When they returned, the pancake was golden and bubbling and I held the pan out to show Captain.

He paused there in the entrance. Hey-Ho's rope fell to the ground. Quiet and slow, Captain walked towards me and crouched at my side by the fire. He said nothing for a while, and even Chips knew something was up because his jaws ceased their perpetual motion.

'I remember,' Captain said eventually, 'my mother making pancakes. She always made pancakes . . .'

I was still fumbling for a reply when Merrick came bursting into Chips's headquarters and out the other side.

'Enemy, sir, massing on the right.'

'Where did the message come from?' we heard the Lieutenant ask. He had two pips now on his shoulder. After Chocolate Hill he'd been made a full Lieutenant and Sparrow was his Second. There were plenty of promotions around after Chocolate Hill, but there was no joy in them.

'Mouth to mouth sir, down the trench, sir.'

'Was that all the message? Was there nothing else?'

There was no answer from Merrick.

'Have you seen anything, Merrick?'

'No, sir.'

Straker called out to Firkins, who was on sentry duty.

'Are you there, Firkins? Can you see anything?'

'No, sir. Nothing, sir.'

We waited tensely in Chips's trench, then since everything seemed to go on much as before, I tipped the pancake on to the plate that Captain held out, smiling. I was relieved about the smiling, and him wanting to eat one, so I set to making another. Chips, having emptied Hey-Ho's cans, was fixing them once more to his side but Hey-Ho had other ideas and was exploring with his muzzle the shelves of provisions in the hope of more biscuit.

Five minutes later we heard Merrick's voice again.

'Enemy massing heavily on our right, sir. Attack expected.'

The Lieutenant called up again to Firkins.

'Can you not see anything? . . . What? Nothing at all? No movement?'

'No, nothing, sir. It's dark, sir.'

At that minute there was the roar and rush of a shell. Hey-Ho reared, wild and whirling with fear, his head hit and lifted the roof of the trench, and the clanging of the metal roof redoubled his terror and he bolted, hurdling Chips's several scattered instruments, his water-cans jangling monstrously in the confined space, and galloped, harness trailing out into the tunnel.

'Fix bayonets, fix bayonets!' Straker was yelling, and the men were all grabbing their rifles, leaping to the parapet, and Captain was making for the door, reaching out for the trailing harness.

'Hey-Ho! Hey-Ho!' he called.

To my horror I heard the din Hey-Ho was making out there in the open – he was going towards the Turkish lines, hoofs pounding on the dry ground, and his cans were clanking and clanging and clashing and making all manner of noises, and the sounds of it all rang through the night and echoed, and that little donkey was raising the noise of a whole cavalry brigade.

There were spurts of fire just beyond our trench.

'Good God!' the Lieutenant yelled, 'They're almost on us – a patrol – right there!'

All the darkness ahead was shot with running fire.

'Twenty of them – thirty of them – Prepare to fire . . . Fire!'

We aimed at the spurts of Jacko's fire that had given his position away and we fired roundly at it until his fire was quenched. When it was quiet, I heard Captain's voice rising from the gully, calling to Hey-Ho. I thought of that terrified donkey, his little legs doing nineteen-to-the-dozen headlong down to the beach, with that terrible ringing in his poor ears wherever he went.

'Doesn't like a shell when it's in a trench,' observed Chips, settling down on his sandbag again. The Lieutenant came into Chips's kitchen just then and he was laughing.

'We'd've been dead to a man – Jacko was almost on us – he was at our door when that little animal went stampeding around. One single animal scared the living daylights out of them – they thought he had the whole British cavalry on them.'

After that, Hey-Ho became a sort of mascot to the unit, but it was Chips who first took to saluting him and Captain. Then they all did, and I think that was their way of recognizing the courage of them both.

Suvla Bay

November 1915

Weeks ran into months and nothing changed, both armies stuck in a stubborn stalemate. We faced each other across perhaps seventeen feet of no man's land. All any of us wanted was to survive and we scratched at that sullen ground and tried to bury ourselves in it. We listened to Johnny Turk's digging, and Johnny Turk listened to ours.

Our summer swims came to an end. For washing now, we were reduced to the bare centimetre of water measured out into our mess tins. Then the dysentery came, and ran like floodwater through our trenches, taking man after man – thirty thousand, they say now, were down with dysentery one time or another.

The days grew biting and cold, and the land took on a melancholy feeling, like that of a wintry Sunday back home. Captain collected blankets and coats and I could sense the deep fear that lay behind the piling up of warm things that was going on in our dugout.

In November the clouds grouped over Gallipoli

and the winds growled around our dugouts. When the storms came, they smashed the piers to splinters. Our machine guns fell out of action, one by one, and the springs on our rifles failed.

Rain fell as if through hosepipes. Sudden torrents poured off the steep slopes and roared down the gorges, turning the hard earth to mud. Our roofs leaked and trenches ran with water. On and on the rain came, raking the graves of the men we'd tried to bury, leaving their bones naked to the skies, washing away their names. The trenches were four foot deep with water in places, and we had to fish bits of food or rifles out of them, and had no dry coats or blankets.

The wind got up, tearing the ships from their anchors, battering and breaking the barges and hurling them ashore. The rain turned to sleet, then hardened to snow. Still our winter uniforms didn't arrive, still we had no greatcoats. It was a terrible time. Men died, right there in the trenches. It was worse for Jacko though, I think, and if we'd been strong enough, we could've just walked over and taken his trenches. Captain was near mute with horror at the cold. It haunted him, brought back memories of other times, and as he retreated into himself, the bruises and the scars in him were easier to see. When the freeze came and the mud turned to ice, men crawled down to the jetties, their feet bound in puttees, black with frostbite. In the early mornings you'd see the rows of dead on the shoreline being sewn up in sacking.

Like two boxers in a ring, the two armies waited. The mail boats swung and pitched and tossed in the bay, unable, for weeks at a time, to come ashore. We felt forgotten and abandoned by the outside world.

A whispered rumour went from trench to trench, tunnel to tunnel, up and down the gullies that spliced those desolate hills. We'd leave. Beasley was laying bets one night as to where we'd be sent: England, the Western Front, perhaps Egypt or the Balkans. The wound Beasley had at Chocolate Hill was healed now after his stint on Moudros, but he wasn't well, and a terrible racking sound came from his chest.

One night, as Captain added another blanket to his pile, I asked, 'Why?'

If we were leaving, why did Captain need so many? His eyes met mine and he hesitated, was about to speak, then shook his head and was silent. It was what had happened before I thought, long ago, that made him so scared of the cold. That was what lay behind the piling up of so many provisions.

Firkins rose and stood, eyes over the parapet, looking towards the Turkish lines, to the ridge, to the new and deadly German guns they'd brought up. How could we ever get away when the Turk gunners had our range to an inch? Captain was there, and I felt his eyes were on me as I laid my bet.

'Wherever we go, we go together, you and me and Hey-Ho,' I said carefully.

I would stay with them, whatever happened. We'd lived together in the crannies of this barren rock, raked by the same heat, the same cold, the same thirst and hunger and illness. Together we'd snatched our food, our water, from the jaws of death. Wherever we went, we'd go together, two boys in a world of men.

It was in December that we received orders to evacuate the peninsula; 83,000 men, 186 guns, everything and everyone to be embarked under cover of night. We'd done the impossible in landing and were now to do the impossible in leaving. There was a sort of guilty anger in all of us then. We'd leave while the blood of the Yeomanry was still wet on the ground, abandon their makeshift graves to the enemy.

Our tents would stay where they were, the candles remain lit. We'd convince Johnny Turk we were digging in for the winter and all the while we'd load our stores secretly on to ships, each night men filing silently down to the beach, packing themselves on to boats and whisking themselves off the peninsula.

The days spent in preparation were cold and anxious. Captain and I were together one afternoon, the two of us crouching in my dugout, peeling the labels off tins of bully, then piercing holes in the tins before sticking the labels back on. The idea was that Johnny Turk would be violently ill when he ate them. I watched Captain carefully. I'd seen him that morning, kneeling, a blanket around his shoulders, at the side of the ruined building at the foot of the cliff. All along the bay, up and down the gullies, he and the other men had been making silent, private visits to the graves of those lost. A gale battered and tore at the scrub around him, and poor Hey-Ho waited, his rear quarters to the wind, muzzle to the stone, shivering violently. I'd noticed how thin the little animal was, his staring knife-edge ribs. We all of us looked like living skeletons that winter, especially the animals.

Captain stuck the label back on, neat and deft always with his fingers, a smile on his face. I always wondered at the smile that came so readily, so easily tickled by the pranks we English liked to play on our enemies, a smile even after a life of so much loss. Recently, though, he'd smiled less than he once had, had been perhaps a little withdrawn, and I thought that sombre mood was because of having to abandon his father here to the wind and rain. Captain had taken to going off alone with Hey-Ho, the pair of them wandering up and down the gullies, Captain's face preoccupied and grave. I noticed too that Captain's pile of blankets and tins had been spirited away, to some other place I supposed, but I thought no more of its disappearance.

Laden with kindling, Hey-Ho was nosing about in

the mud and snow for the thistles that were now all sodden and brown.

'Hey-Ho!'

The little donkey raised his head at Captain's voice and trotted up. I smiled at the sweetness of him but Captain's mouth tightened and he shook his head very slightly. He rose and went to Hey-Ho, and bent his head, his eyes closing, his forehead lowered to Hey-Ho's, and they stood together, nose to nose for a long while.

The next day the Lieutenant set us to rigging up rifles so as to keep them firing after we'd deserted the trench. Captain was quicker than me with his hands, would make a good engineer, I thought. We'd made booby traps too, to blow up the dugouts when Johnny Turk opened the door. I watched Captain placing one can above another next to a rifle, the top full of water and set to drip into the other. When the bottom one was full, its weight would pull the wire tight around the rifle's trigger and fire it. Captain smiled at the schoolboy contraption.

'We'll be the rear, Captain,' I said proudly. 'The Yeomen will be among the last to leave Gallipoli.' I'd asked the Lieutenant if I could be the very last to leave. I felt there was some honour in that, in being the last man up there, and I wanted to prove to the others I was man enough to do it. You see, one man in every sector of the hill had had to stay behind right up to the very last minute to set up the rifles. Lieutenant Sparrow had agreed, but I noticed that when Straker heard, his lips tightened as though he thought I were the wrong choice.

Captain's eyes dropped to the wire he was wrapping around the trigger of a rifle.

'Hey-Ho makes more noise than all of them . . .' He looked up at me. 'The mules that make most noise will stay right to the end, to make the enemy think we are all still here.'

I heard the choke in his throat but thought Captain was worried only by the same fear I had, that we'd be somehow left behind, abandoned to Johnny Turk.

'It's an honour,' I said stubbornly, 'to be last to leave.'

We all of us in the following days were tense, and as the shadows of the last day lengthened, we were jumpy as June bugs. There was something steely in the set of Captain's face that I'd not seen before.

I had an important role to play in the leaving of Gallipoli that night and I was full of that, and anxious, so I wasn't thinking too much just then about Captain or Hey-Ho. In the late afternoon, when Firkins and Merriman were tying sandbags round their feet and Lieutenant Sparrow laying sandbags along the floor to muffle our footsteps, Captain rose to leave the trench. He walked over to me.

'You will be all right,' he said. 'The boats will wait for you.' I thought then that he knew how scared I was to stay on at the top of the hill and man all the rifles till the very last minute, while he was down on the beach, with Hey-Ho there, making a racket beside him, with all the boats at very close hand.

'My friend,' he said. 'Good luck.'

'Good luck,' I answered. 'See you on the boat.'

Captain didn't answer. He looked at me searchingly, paused, seemed to be on the point of saying something, then bit his lip and hesitated before turning quickly to make his way with Hey-Ho down to the beach.

I stood a while dithering and feeling strangely lost.

You will be all right. The boats will wait for you.

Captain's words played in my head but I didn't stop to think why they bothered me.

Robins and Chips began to light the little cooking fires along the trench as though it were a night like any other. One by one, a thousand other little cooking fires were lit, up and down the hill. The stars were bright, the night strangely peaceful.

The minutes crept on.

The hope that we'd get away swelled with every passing hour. Sometimes Johnny Turk attacked at dawn, sometimes at night. If he came now, he'd scupper all our plans. I was with Firkins, in Chips's kitchen, filling my water bottle and collecting iron rations. Firkins was as jumpy and on edge as me, and when the Sergeant-Major's face appeared suddenly round the sacking door at the far end of our sector, we both leaped out of our skins.

'Lieutenant Straker. Word passed to you, sir, to march.'

The moment had come for them all to go and I'd be left alone in this part of the trench with all the ghosts of the men who'd gone, and the blood-soaked land all around, and the Turkish lines so close.

The Lieutenant nodded. Another officer appeared.

'Sir, take your men over the table-land and wait on the beach.'

The Lieutenant paused in surprise, before nodding. The table-land was high, and exposed to all the Turkish guns, and he'd have preferred to take the sheltered gully. In silence, each man was preparing to leave. Lieutenant Straker took me aside and whispered.

'Man the rifles, Bayliss, all twelve. Hold the position at all costs. Remain alert at all times. Don't move till three a.m.' He gave my shoulder an encouraging squeeze. 'You'll be all right, Billy.'

He turned to address the men and mouthed, 'D Company. March.'

Merriman picked up a pencil and paper and wrote something. The company of twenty-eight filed out in silence, threading through the trench on padded feet, eyes to the ground, a friendly hand on my shoulder as each passed, and I felt proud to be the one to stay, proud as well as scared.

'No talking now, no smoking,' whispered Straker to each man at the door.

As he left, Merrick tacked up his note to the lintel:

AU REVOIR, ABDUL

I smiled to see that. We respected Johnny Turk, all of us, him being a good and fair fighter.

I was left alone with all the tiny fires and all the poisoned bully beef and the twelve rifles and if Jacko came over now, creeping and silent as a cat, it would be only me, only me in all this empty tunnel, to face his bayonets.

I moved along the trench, lighting a candle in each dugout. I had to make as much noise as possible while I was in the trench, and Captain and Hey-Ho would be on the beach, going to and fro, squeaking and barking and being noisy and trying to make the noise of ten donkeys, but they would be close to the jetties and the boats, and they wouldn't be forgotten or left behind.

I leaped with fright at a sudden sound, stood rooted to the spot, every sense straining. Muffled footsteps – our own – just another column of men – the Australians, perhaps, from the sector to our left. We were still all a bit in awe of the Australians, and their swaggering, easy ways, and I wished I were going down with them. While Hey-Ho and the donkeys on the beach were busy making a racket, the men abandoning the trenches had to keep silent as snakes so that Jacko would think we were still in them. I checked the slow and creeping hands of my watch. The sappers, I told myself, were up here too in the trench beyond, and they'd be the only ones to leave later than me. Only once they'd lit the fuses to detonate the mines could they leave.

Moonlight shone spookily through the entrances on to each rifle position. The minutes crawled by, slower than any minutes I'd ever known. I bent to retie the rags around my boots once again. There were more footsteps, the ghostly tramp of another column of men moving through the support trench.

I checked my watch one last time. 2.50 a.m. My nerves gave out just then, at 2.50 a.m., and I moved along the line of rifles, filling each water-can with a trembling hand. At 2.55 I abandoned the position and got myself as fast and as silently down the loose, slipping scree of that near-vertical track as it's possible to do in a state of abject terror.

At the foot of the cliff I ran into a mass of men, huddled together and shivering. The darkness was thick with whispered commands and muffled tramping feet. I asked after D Company and was indicated to the third jetty. A figure stood marshalling men on to a lighter. Breathless, heart still pounding, I got there as the last man embarked.

'Hurry, Bayliss,' said Lieutenant Straker, but I heard the relief in his voice that I'd made it.

Instinctively I scanned the faces on the boat, looking for Captain. Very slowly a single, staring fact dawned on me. My stomach lurched: there were no animals – not on this boat, nor on any other. Hey-Ho! *Hey-Ho!* – Where was he? How were they getting out? Where were they all? All the valiant creatures who'd gone up and down those gullies for us with their heavy loads, and nothing but thistle and army biscuit to eat, hour after hour, up the scree, down the scree . . . Where were they, and how would they get away? I cast my head around wildly.

'Where's Captain, sir? Where are they?'

'Bayliss. Get aboard.'

Captain's strained and anxious face flashed before me. I remembered the strange hug he'd given me and my gut twisted.

Lieutenant Straker looked up at the sky, then down at his watch. The waves moaned softly around the lighter.

'Where are they, sir?'

He shook his head, as if despairing of such nonsense at such at time.

'Get aboard, Bayliss.'

'No, sir,' I said, shaking my head. 'No.'

'As your senior officer, I command you to board.'

I scanned the faces of the men on the lighter once more, face after face, all filthy, haggard, lean and weary. No Captain – of course not, not if Hey-Ho weren't here.

The Lieutenant pulled me aside.

'For God's sake, Billy,' he hissed. He caught me by the arm. 'Captain's not here . . . The animals aren't – they're – they've . . .'

I looked at him, slack-mouthed, sick with horror.

'Did you not know? Didn't he tell you?'

I pulled away, took a step backwards down the jetty.

Captain had never told me the animals were to be left behind. Perhaps he thought I'd known. Did he not trust me? Was that why he'd said nothing?

The Lieutenant grabbed my arm.

'Billy, we can't – the Army can't . . . can't get the animals off—'

'Where? Where are they, sir? Where are they?'

Wherever Hey-Ho was, Captain would be.

'For God's sake, get aboard . . . Look, it's too late—'

'What d'you mean, it's too late? What do you mean?' I mouthed, silent with horror.

He stretched out an arm towards the northern end of the bay, but didn't turn his head in that direction. Very slowly I turned mine and looked. Gradually I made out dark mounds, row after row of them, the dark blood of them staining the shingle and running down into the water. I reeled – their throats slit – cut with a knife so they'd die in silence – Hey-Ho? No, no, no, surely not – his throat slit? – No – no, not that, not his throat, not Hey-Ho, not . . .

The Lieutenant released my arm, took a step away from me and barked, 'Bayliss, get aboard. That is an order.'

I took another step backwards, then another.

'That is an order, Bayliss.'

'Damn orders,' said a voice in the boat. 'Damn orders.' Chips rose to his feet. 'The boy comes with us.'

'Get aboard, Bayliss,' the Lieutenant said again, his eyes on me.

'Every drop of water we drank—' Chips continued.

'It's an order, Bayliss,' the Lieutenant interrupted.

'Goddamn orders . . .' said Chips.

'No, sir,' I mouthed to Straker.

He grabbed me by the shoulders.

'I order you, Bayliss, on to that boat.'

'Damn orders,' said a voice I recognized as Firkins's, then Merriman and Robins and Beasley said it too, and a whispered chant was taken up down the ranks of waiting men sitting in that boat. One by one they rose to their feet.

'Captain comes with us. Captain comes with us.' Some looked uneasily up to the sky, but still they whispered. 'Captain comes with us.'

Straker caught me by the hand and whispered, 'It's too late, Billy – Can't you see? Not without . . . he won't come, wouldn't come without . . .'

As the chant continued from the boat, the muscles of Straker's jaw tightened. They seemed to quiver and he whipped his head round and grabbed me and hissed, 'Damn you, Bayliss, for this insubordinate behaviour. Five minutes, I give you *five* minutes to find him. After five minutes we leave.'

Where would he be?

'Please God, please God,' I whispered to myself as I spun around, 'please let me find him . . .'

He'd not be up in the hills, he'd not surrender – Johnny Turk was gallant in a fight but you wouldn't want to be taken prisoner by him. We'd all seen what he could do to a prisoner.

I paused midway up the beach, careless of the unwinding rags on my boots. Would he be at his father's grave? I raced, frantic, to the far end of the bay. If it wasn't too late he'd be . . . he'd be where the ruins were, where his father was buried.

I found Captain. He was in the ruined building at the foot of the gully at the northern end of the bay. He was there, alone at the back of the building, in the dark, quaking with fear at the sound of approaching footsteps. Behind him stood Hey-Ho and Captain's arms were stretched out, one to the donkey's head, the other to his rump, and his fingers were trembling and quaking and clutching at Hey-Ho's silver fur. The little donkey, squeezed between his master and the sheet rock of the cliff, was muzzled in a strip of Army blanket, his hoofs bound in sandbags. Despite the unusual circumstances and the strange wrappings on him, there was no fear in him. He was with his master and all was well with his world.

'Captain . . .' I said.

Like a wild cat he looked at me. He was coiled tense as a spring, chest rising and falling. He'd thought perhaps I was the enemy creeping up on him, or a British General come to slit Hey-Ho's throat. I stepped forward, searching in my pocket for the biscuit I knew would be there. I stretched out my hand to Hey-Ho, who stretched out his head to me, and I eased the muzzle just enough to let him eat.

'The boat is waiting,' I whispered to Hey-Ho.

Captain looked steadily at me and slowly moved his head from side to side.

'We stay, Hey-Ho and I stay, together,' he said, his voice shaky but determined.

'Well, we will miss the boat then, all three of us . . .'

Behind Captain, provisions were stacked on a ledge of rock. He'd been planning to stay on here, he and Hey-Ho alone on this savage shore with only a small stash of tinned food and a large number of blankets.

'Because if we have to swim to Moudros, that's

what we will do. I will not go without you both. But right now, there happens to be a boat waiting for you both, and for us all.'

A single tear slipped down Captain's cheek.

'Quickly,' I added.

Lieutenant Straker had rigged up a pair of broad planks to the lighter. One ear forward, one back, Hey-Ho stepped on to it, calm and easy as you please.

'Insubordinate hooligans, the pair of you boys,' Straker hissed, watching Hey-Ho's picky, tippy-toed gait up the planks. But I knew he was relieved – relieved and happy and surprised.

Each man in that boat was standing, each man held a hand to his cap in a long and silent salute. The Lieutenant's eyes rose to the sky, still wary of the creeping dawn, but there was a smile on his face as he gave me a great shove on to the boat to hurry me. Men held out fistfuls of chocolate, biscuit, cigarettes, even as Hey-Ho tiptoed calmly between them, stopping to eat from each palm, making his way determinedly to the prow, having evidently decided on that as the most interesting option available. Captain followed, smiling through his tears.

The rope was loosed. We turned and pulled away.

As we left the bay, the Lieutenant checked his watch and nodded to us, and we all of us turned to the stern, men pushing towards the deck rails. In silence we watched the surf break on the shingle. Something of us all was left behind at Gallipoli, but for me it was my boyhood that lay shredded on the white shingle, fallen from me and lost like something dropped from a pocket.

The Lieutenant checked his watch one last time and looked up, and I saw the sudden explosion of a mine, then another, and another, the hills erupting in a display of fireworks. The Turk guns spurted with fire We turned to one another and smiled grimly. We'd landed on that unapproachable coast, over water that was wired and mined, in the face of enemy fire, we'd attacked uphill an impregnable natural fortress, we'd been outnumbered at every moment but we'd taken the beach. And we'd stayed there.

A tent went up in flames, then another, and another, and then they were going up in their hundreds, the guy ropes wavering, the canvas loose and floating up like storybook ghosts. The stacks of stores on the beaches went up and soon the whole coast was one immense flame, and every Turkish gun was firing to stop the attack they thought was coming.

I turned to the prow. The boat slipped through the starry sea, the moon broke through the clouds and smiled and it seemed that we were moving away into a better world. I saw Hey-Ho's four neat hoofs braced against the boards, the tips of his ears silvered in the moonshine, his long head towards the open sea.

I wasn't guilty then, not at Gallipoli.

I don't like to look back, for the remorse that it brings, but if I do, I see Captain there on the boat, and I see the trust I'd won, shining and lucent in his face.

PART III

SINAI

Rafa (and other terrible places)

1916

Gallipoli was only the start of it all.

We returned to Egypt and to Mena and to the Yeomanry horses. All the sounds of Egypt, the singing of the frogs and the creaking of waterwheels, and the warmth of it, were balmy and familiar after the cold of Gallipoli.

At sundown on our second day there, when the Mokattam hills grew pink as Bredicot roses, the villages all adrift on silvery floodwater, their domes and minarets glowing white beneath the purple sky, we rode out together, Captain on Hey-Ho, I on a tall dark mare. The motion of that mare was silky and smooth; not as smooth as Trumpet, but I think I was showing off a little, what with her high step and fine ways, and I galloped ahead so that Captain might admire her. I knew that donkeys don't gallop – Captain had told me that a donkey must go at his own pace – but even at a walk, Hey-Ho, like any other donkey, was faster than a horse, and that pinched a mean nerve in me.

When I turned, he and Hey-Ho had already headed home.

At Mena we were near the railway, and there was mail for almost all of us. We formed a scrum around the mail station, Captain waiting, as always, at a distance and alone. There was an envelope for me, blotched and half disintegrated, across it the words:

SAVED FROM THE SEA

Captain was delighted by the miracle of that small envelope fished out of the sea, and he was beaming for me.

'From Liza,' I told him.

Dear Billy,
I wish you were better at writing letters.
    I am learning about the pyramids in Geography.
I am glad Trumpet did not go to war with you.
Trumpet is not at all the right sort of horse to take
into a war. He likes clover and cow parsley and
I know there is none in Egypt. Mother says the
Egyptians are fearfully horrid to animals. She also
says she is glad you are not in France, that it's much
worse there. Did you know Francis has finished
school now? He is very bossy to us all.
    Geordie says he is going to sign up and go to war
like you, but that he will go to a proper war like the

one in France, not a small thing in the Middle East where you are only fighting Turks. Francis says that is not the same thing at all as fighting Germans.

Abel Rudge said you were having an easy time of it in Gallipoli, and Mother said that was just as well. She doesn't talk about you much but she is always reading the newspapers so I think she does mind a bit.

Francis says he will have Geordie horsewhipped if Geordie so much as tries to go to war and Geordie cries when Francis says that. Geordie still doesn't come up higher than the sideboard in the kitchen and he can't tie his shoelaces, so the Army wouldn't want him anyway, but he pulls a face if you tell him that. Here is some clover from the field for the horse they give you as I can't imagine what the Army is feeding them on.

Try to write soon,

Love, Liza

Later, Captain went to the canteen and bought a postcard.

'Write,' he said simply, handing it to me. 'Write to your family.'

He watched me as I sat scratching my head and wondering what on earth I could say to Liza, when really there were so many things I could have written about.

'What is it like?' Captain asked. 'Inside your house?' Then as I picked up the pen again, he asked, 'Is there a kitchen? Are there tables and chairs?'

I didn't tell him there were tables, and rooms for the winter, and rooms for the summer, and a room for breakfast, another room for music, a library . . . Later Captain asked what colour the cows were, and if there were more horses or just Trumpet. He could go on and on asking about my home but there was no self-pity in the asking even though in all the world he had only what he stood up in, only that and Hey-ho.

I told Liza that the newspapers said we Yeomen were the 'most stalwart soldiers Britain has ever sent forth from her shores' and that she was to be sure to tell Mother and Francis and Geordie that. Also to tell Abel Rudge that the Turk was a gentleman, and a gallant fighter, but that he didn't have the stomach for a bayonet fight. Then I scratched that last bit out with lots of ink and told Liza to tell Abel Rudge, too, that France was a stalemate and all the men there like rats in holes and in Egypt it would all be big open fighting and great charges at breakneck speed. I never told Liza about marching forward over the bodies of the dead and the wounded, or the flies and sand that got into their wounds as they lay out in the sun, crying like children for water.

After this I was at a place called Oghratina. We were caught out there, mired in soft, deep sand, three and a half thousand Turks swooping down on us in a surprise attack screaming out to Allah. They always had the water, you see, so their infantry moved three times as fast as ours. Our wounded lay out there, delirious with sun and thirst, sinking into the sand, an arm rising here and there, begging for water.

At Katia it was bad too. There at Katia, we were mad with thirst, each of us ready to cut the throat of another to get water. Captain and Hey-Ho crossed no man's land to reach us, climbed dunes, fetlock-deep in that scorching sand while all around them the artillery roared and screamed. We formed a scrum around them, fighting each other to get at it, pouring it into helmets or hands, spilling it in our hurry. Captain and little Hey-Ho went about among us till there was no more water to bring up. Someone told the Lieutenant that there was water two foot under the sand by the palm trees and we dug for it with our bare hands, scrabbling for it like dogs.

It was the Lieutenant that made sure, ever since Gallipoli, that Captain and Hey-Ho were looked after, that they were attached to Chips and to the mess section, and followed wherever we Yeomen went.

At El Bitia we rested and swam in the sea every day, a whole regiment of us, all wrestling and playing war games in the sparkling water. We had bell tents and pyjamas and tables to eat at, and in the evenings Captain and I would make *café au lait*, smoke cigarettes and lie on our backs, looking up at the moon. We'd talk about the things we wanted to do one day, the men we wanted to be. Just then, too, Captain was interested in the funny words we English use and we'd list them. He'd start, out of the blue with 'Collywobbles'. He always started with that. 'Collywobbles' amused him more than any of them.

I'd answer, 'Clobber.'

'Canoodle.'

'Mollycoddle.'

'Fuddy-duddy.'

And so we'd go on, and I'd have to rack my brains to think of more. We'd talk mostly, though, about the food we dreamed of eating.

'Pancakes,' Captain would always say. That was always top of his list. My list was very long, and the first time I told him the things I longed for he looked at me with bewilderment: toad-in-the-hole, bubble-and-squeak, jam roly-poly . . .

We never talked about the things we'd seen, about the bodies of the dead or the battles. Captain was happy there at El Bitia in the sun and the sea, and with Hey-Ho growing strong and round again.

'Why did you come to Egypt?' I asked him once. We were lying on our backs on the beach, a band somewhere playing a tune from Gilbert and Sullivan.

'They made a camp for us there and we had nowhere else to go.'

His people had been chased out of Russia and Eastern Europe and all places, booted from one place to another, until they'd thrown in their lot with the English when the war broke out. Long before the war, Captain had known the violence that men can have in their hearts. His father had taught him – his own life had taught him – to trust only family, only kith and kin. Hey-Ho was all that was left to him of that. For Captain, there was only family and Hey-Ho, and in all the world, I was the only exception to this rule.

Too soon we were moved from El Bitia to Romani, and that was a hard-fought battle. We had orders not to drink till noon. I never told Liza about how it was at Romani, and I hope she and Mother never read in the papers about how bad it was there. How the horses had no water and were staggering from the want of it, how we'd stumbled back, finding our way in the dark through the sand, past carts, columns of prisoners, camels and mounted troops, fighting our way to the troughs.

Sometime later the pack-animals came in. Hey-Ho's head was tired and low, his feet sore. Flies clustered in the corners of his eyes but he hadn't the strength to blink them away as Captain fed and watered him. There was a train of camels approaching to water, too. Captain watched them.

'A camel is good for here,' he said, stroking Hey-Ho. 'Better.'

When they came in to water I eyed their loose, slavering lips and baggy, wrinkled chins, and all the primitive intelligence of those prehistoric and savage heads, and wondered at Captain's thinking.

There were no tents that night, and no blankets, and we slept in holes we dug in the ground. From there we went on, and the going was terrible for the horses, the sand soft and deep, and my mare was in up to her fetlocks at every step. Poor Hey-Ho, somewhere, would be in up to his knees. Then, from whatever place it was we got to that day, we had to push straight on. No rest or sleep at all. We trekked all through the night, navigating by the stars, only to find at the next place that Jacko had retreated, and we had to chase on after him. Liza would have wept to see the state of the horses that morning, to hear they had to go on another twenty-five miles. By dawn we had the next place, and its stinking wells, but two nights later we were on the move again. There was no water, you see, until we reached Maghdaba, so we had no choice but to keep going. In silence but for the jingling of harness and firearms, we set off again over those sand waves, ocean after unending ocean of them.

When dawn came and scraped away the stars, we were in sight of whatever garrison it was we were after. We circled the stronghold while Jacko went scrambling around in his pyjamas to mount the guns in his redoubts. I didn't know where Captain was, if he'd come up yet or not, nor how Hey-Ho would have coped with so many long marches, one after another through the night.

'Dismount!'

A dismounted attack.

When you're on a horse, he dances and jigs and strikes the ground, carries you forward, knee to knee, caught up in the rolling wave of the whole thing, and it's the horse that takes you forward, whether you like it or not but it's not the same at all if you're on foot, it would be my own legs, my own will that would have to take me onward, one foot in front of the other.

After a twenty-mile night march, we left our exhausted mounts and trudged up on foot, with rifle and bayonet, towards a natural fortress held by a well-armed enemy. We formed a line and prepared to attack.

'Bayonets out! Advance!'

My fear of a dismounted attack was tempered that day by my exhaustion, I think, because I went forward with the others, though I didn't cheer as they did.

Jacko's fire was a wonder that morning. It spun mercifully high over head, hopelessly high. He was marvellously sleepy and erratic, and our bayonets rattled from one end of the line to the other, and glinted in the sun, and we made a race of it, dashing over the open ground, and one by one white flags appeared in the redoubts and the day was ours.

Somehow or other I got through, and I never used that bayonet.

We watered the horses at the wells in front of the wadi and turned their faithful, drooping heads back to El Arish. For the third night we went without sleep. Slumped in my saddle, I trusted my mare to follow the straggling train, a line that stretched as far as you could see across the horizon. The Service Corps didn't catch up with us that night, but I hoped that somewhere out in that dark night Captain would be walking beside Hey-Ho and that he'd be wondering where I was and how I'd fared that day.

That year, 1916, was all like that: long night treks, one skirmish after another. We were on the move all the time, and Captain and I were often apart, each at the far end of the ghostly trains that moved across the desert sands, but there are two moments that stand out, two moments that chart the changes in our friendship.

I'd been sent out on reconnaissance, somewhere to the east, because an English officer and four Yeomen had been killed. I had to go with Ballard and twenty others. The Lieutenant allocated us Captain and Hey-Ho to carry provisions. Our mission was to scour the wadis and the hills for Turks.

We'd crossed a wretched piece of country, all rocks and holes, and were bivouacked right in the grip of the hills. Captain was picking scrub with his own hands and carrying it to Hey-Ho. Hey-Ho had lost condition again, was painfully thin; we all were, all of us, men and animals being on one-third rations just then. One ship after another had gone down, our food supplies, our mail, all lost. I was sitting with Merriman and this chap Ballard, and we were talking of cricket scores and hunting. I saw Captain pause and watch me, hearing all the Englishness of the English, and the small things of home that drew me to those men. I was turning more and more, you see, towards the men with whom the ties of country and county made companionship a ready, easy thing. Captain stood there, apart, in the darkness by the animals, a refugee, a camp follower, with no rank and no official role. He was carrying bits of grassy stalks to my mare. When the talk turned to hand-to-hand fighting, I felt Captain glance at me; he knew me as Merriman and Ballard never would. He knew that though I could turn a rifle on a man, I was paralysed by the bayonet. You see, you're right up close with a bayonet, and it's a different thing altogether than using a rifle because you can see the other man's face, you can see the fear in his eyes, and well, I just couldn't use the thing. But I turned my face away from Captain, and when Merriman laughed, I laughed, and Ballard laughed, and I made out that I could use a bayonet and kill with it and laugh about it afterwards.

There's another moment, too, that I remember, one that wakes me in the night and turns me clammy with shame, a moment that worms its way into even the most sunny moment and wrings me to a twisted rag. When I think of Captain now, I think of this moment as much as what came after. It was at Rafa. We'd done a night ride up there so as to catch Jacko in his pyjamas again at dawn. We had the Cameliers on our right, they were mostly Australians, the New Zealanders to our left – and they're both fine folks to have with you in a battle. The enemy had a clear field of fire in every direction and we were making heavy weather of it, but the New Zealanders made a charge across a grassy slope and then we all pressed on the attack. It was a mounted charge – I had a fresh horse then, a young gelding, and I was alongside Merrriman and Robins, three veterans of Gallipoli together. The Lieutenant had detailed the three of us to ride as a unit and to take one of the redoubts. It was a mounted attack and so I was caught up in the rolling wave of the charge, buoyed up by the courage of the other men, and their blood was hot, singing for the thrill of it all and they were laughing and shouting. Anyway, we were away, our arms glittering in the sun, hoofs thundering and pounding the dry ground, and we went at those Turks hard and fast; and I thought as I rode how poor Captain would be somewhere in the mess lines, with the donkeys and the water-cans, while

I galloped a tall fine gelding in a big open charge.

We went so fast that morning that Jacko couldn't alter his machine-gun sights in time to catch us – we were going right in under them and his fire was mostly hopeless and high above our heads. But Merriman went down, and Robins. I turned and hailed a medic. I thought I saw Captain and Hey-Ho, and I saw Merriman's mare beside Robins's mount, and the two of them were riderless and they'd paused together and turned for the back lines. Without Merriman or Robins, it was up to me alone to take the redoubt, the German Maxim and the dead-eyed gunner manning it; up to me alone to dismount, if necessary, and take it at point of bayonet. The Lieutenant was motioning me on to that redoubt and on I went.

I got to the mouth of the redoubt. I held that bayonet and at the entrance, I paused and gripped it and steeled myself. I went in and thought at first that there was no one there – that they'd abandoned position and that I wouldn't have to use the bayonet, that I would just mount and ride on to the rifle pits. Then I saw, strapped to the gun, a young Turk, with staring ribs and eyes. He was no more than a boy, and he was strapped to that gun, tied to it with rope by his German masters. Even to me that boy was young, perhaps no more than twelve, and he was ragged and starving. The bayonet turned to lead in my hands.

I never saw the German right behind me till he

fell. I turned when I heard a shot and then saw him slump to the ground. There behind him was Captain on Merriman's mare, his rifle levelled. I waited while Captain galloped up.

'Captain . . .' I said, and with my arm I pointed to the child at the gun.

We both looked at him then, and Captain hesitated. He was a child, ragged and starving and convulsed with fear. Captain caught my gelding's reins and led him to me. I mounted and we turned away from that child, both of us, at the same time, and went on.

I was commended for gallantry, after Rafa; given a medal that I never felt was mine to take or wear. Captain was proud for me, but there was a wariness, too, if the medal caught his attention. He looked often, searchingly, at me, wondering, I think now, what kind of friend I'd be, whether distinctions and honours would force a wedge between us.

'Father . . .' he said once, around about this time. 'Father had a medal too.' There was some pride in his voice and also some hurt. I remembered the plummy officer who'd torn his father's stripes from his arm and ground them into the dirt of the horse lines outside Alexandria. I remembered Captain, too, on the beach, sewing them back on to his father's sleeve by starlight, on the night he buried him.

We'd been all the other had in the way of a

companion. Friendships made in war are forged and tested in heat that is white hot. You are under a microscope when you're living at such close quarters, the good and the bad of you open for all to see.

That whole episode at Rafa and the medal made me ashamed, and I think it was after that that I began to grow shifty with Captain, shifty as the wind of Arabia, turning to him or turning away as it suited me.

It was about this time, too, because of the medal perhaps, that men like Ballard and Skerret and Hadley took up with me. I was silly, flattered to be taken up by them, but I felt grand, too, and thought I knew what it felt like to be a man when I was with them. They were older even than Francis, and when you're young you count out carefully the years between yourself and the men you look up to.

Gaza

1917

In Sinai, Firkins took to talking about Samson and the Philistines, and how we were in the wilderness. Of course we could all see that without Firkins saying anything about it, but he kept on about how beyond Gaza there'd be fig trees and vines and flowers and milk and honey. We groaned and rolled our eyes but we had a terrible time of it at Gaza. We had two pitiful and bungled attempts at it. The second time we attacked Gaza was the same as the first – all choking dust and blinding sun. You can't think, you see, when it's like that, when the enemy is blanketed in smoke, and sand is spurting up and the men and horses around you are writhing and screaming. I was still on that young gelding at Gaza, and he was caught by shrapnel and that sent him rearing up, poor chap. I fell from him as he spun and fled wildly, reins trailing, for the back lines.

I staggered back, step by sinking step, mirage and madness mixed in me, reeling like a drunk in the soft sand, foaming at the mouth like a wild dog. Thirst is most agonizing at sundown and in the back lines I scrambled for the water on my hands and knees like a beast. My gelding was there with the Veterinary Corps, already bandaged, and Captain and Hey-Ho were there too in the back lines, going among the men who were naked and delirious, their tongues black and swollen.

It was a terrible journey from there back to the Wadi Ghuzzee, heads aching from the sun, eyes bloodshot with the blinding glare that came off the sand, stragglers falling and left to die in our wake, the blind linking arms, the whole desert and sky the colour of dust, the dust so thick you could lose sight of the horse in front. Only by listening could I tell where the camels were, the mules, the limbers, the artillery wagons and all the rattling paraphernalia of war.

In the dusk of the second day, the sky turned lurid, the light strange and fitful. A hot wind blew in, the heat of it increasing minute by minute till it had the blast of a furnace. My gelding was a noble thing and he never played up with me for nothing. When an immense cloud came at us, huge and gauzy, he dug his hoofs in and shook and quivered and pawed the sand. Officers were charging down the lines, their tempers ragged, urging us on. That cloud was coming towards us at a licking pace. My gelding put his head down and whimpered, and all around us men were cowering, and suddenly we were in the teeth of a storm, a hurricane-force wind, heavy with sand. I thought of Liza and the paddock with the elderly apple tree, in the lee of the westerly breezes. I was glad Liza couldn't see then how the horses suffered, their eyes bloodshot and weeping with sand, their blind and stumbling attempts to move. I lashed that gelding and tried to turn him, the sand burning like needles on my face and arms and hands. He bunched together with the other horses, all of them shoulder to shoulder, nose to tail, in a tight knot, some forwards, some backwards. He moaned and dropped his head away from the whip and sting of the sand.

'Billy . . . Billy!'

Captain and Hey-Ho were there, in the swirling sand beside us, an arrangement of blanket around the donkey's eyes and silver muzzle, his nose buried between Captain's back and arm.

'Billy, wait!'

Captain tied a strip of shirt around my gelding's muzzle while I fell helplessly over her neck, sand in my eyes and mouth and nose. Hey-Ho tripped on doggedly, neck extended so as to keep his muzzle buried in the pit of Captain's arm. He went wherever Captain led, through storms of sand, storms of shrapnel, on he went at his master's side, Captain his alpha and his omega. We followed, the muzzle of my gelding to Hey-Ho's salt-and-pepper tail, on and on, till we reached a gully and flung ourselves down and staggered blindly, vomiting to a patch of scrub.

We dug at the sand and stone with our bare fingers while the swirling wind struck at our limbs and tore the clothes from our backs and lashed our skin raw with grit and sand and drew trickles of blood from our skin. We crouched together, Captain and I, in the shallow scoop we'd made, blankets over our heads.

The wind grew still more violent, shifting the waves of sand from one place to another, flooding our dugout and forcing us away. In the dead of the night we staggered, clutching each other, to where the animals stood bunched. They had no shelter, their flanks and necks, poor things, streaked with blood drawn through their skin by the lashing sand.

It was after that sandstorm that we were camping near to the Wadi Ghuzzee, our tail between our legs, licking our wounds after that second attempt on Gaza. We were all in and around the Ghuzzee, the infantry to our left, Camel Corps to our right, the Hun planes overhead. That wadi was a shocking place, flies in our drink, in our food, and we had to sleep amidst all the creeping, crawling things of Arabia, but there were dates and porridge and jam and bread.

It was there, on our last night in the Ghuzzee, that Ballard called out, 'Bayliss, young Bayliss, over here!'

I was standing on my own in the canteen, queuing to buy pears and cocoa and half listening to Ballard and Skerret's banter.

'Bayliss, over here!'

Captain was waiting for me, perhaps grooming Hey-Ho. Captain was at Hey-Ho's side all the time there in the Wadi Ghuzzee, worried that Hey-Ho was losing condition, a hand on the drooping ear.

'Come on, Bayliss,' said Firkins and Hadley.

They were determined to make a night of it. Tomorrow we'd rise at four and move north again. We'd make another attempt on Gaza, but this time we'd surprise Jacko and hit him first at Beersheba, where he wouldn't expect us.

Ballard had a parcel from home: chocolate and the *Malvern Gazette*. I sat with them and we read of all the little things of home, of the inches of rain and the appointment of a new mayor, till all the Englishness of England and all the wet of Worcestershire were swimming in my head; and I never went to Captain with the pears and cocoa.

In the morning we breakfasted on biscuit and bully and sipped from our water bottles.

My new mare was saddled and bridled, her nose in a bag of corn, Captain at her side. He lifted her head, held a wet cloth and held it to her muzzle.

'The smell of water, just the smell of it, will help her thirst,' he said. The terrible memories of the last two attempts on Gaza were in his mind's eye too that morning. He held out his hand to me.

'This is for you.'

He placed a pebble in my palm. I half laughed, not knowing what it was for and wondering if it was because I'd offended him that he was giving me such a thing, but he laughed too, easily and freely.

'Suck it,' he said. 'When your mouth is dry, keep it there and suck it.' He'd learned that from the Arab syces – the native grooms – who looked after the transport camels – like all desert people, they knew to suck stones to keep the mouth wet. I only smiled back at him as I took the pebble. There was guilt in my silence, you see, because I was thinking how I'd never taken him the pears and cocoa, and how I'd shared them instead with Ballard and the others.

'Good luck,' Captain said, and then I knew he didn't mind about petty things because he smiled and said, 'Here are some more, for your friends.'

When the sun rose we were in position and in full order. The big guns were brought forward at a gallop. We Yeomen waited in line while our shells began to roar and flash and screech across the sky. Then Jacko's guns roared too, and shells were screeching in all directions, rolls of sound splitting the air, the red earth erupting, the hills roaring and crashing with them. The field artillery began to snap and bark, and the noise was beyond bearing, beyond all imagining. The infantry moved forward and everywhere men were moving, columns of red dust rising, officers yelling, but we were still to wait and watch in the shelter of a dry watercourse.

Bullets *whiss-whiss-whissed* and *zip-zipped* into the sand around the infantry, shrapnel bursting in clouds that opened and grew loose and soft as dandelions.

All day we waited and watched, and I rolled that pebble around in my mouth and held the cloth to my mare's muzzle. As the day wore on, and the heat and thirst grew, each of us still there, each holding a weary, thirsty horse, we began to turn our eyes to Beersheba where the wells were.

I eyed the sprawling houses of the town, and the pepper trees and the eucalyptus, and thought of the cool deep water in her wells. I uncorked and sipped the last from my bottle. My mare whinnied at the scent of water and the thrust of her head threw me almost to the ground. The afternoon was slipping away, but there could be no retreat. The water was either thirty miles behind or three miles in front. And eleven thousand horses must drink or die.

Of a sudden there was a distant drumming and shouting, and Lieutenant Straker said, 'Good God! The Australians – they've no swords – at bayonet – they're . . .'

A brigade of mounted men wearing the emu

feathers of the Australian Light Horse crested a ridge and moved across the plain at a hard gallop amid splashes of sand and flame, and leaping clouds of dust. The infantry had been going a bit slow for their liking and they hadn't waited around for forms to be signed or instructions to be given, they'd just fixed their bayonets and tucked their rifles under their right armpits and taken their chances and set off. We felt the pounding of their hoofs beneath our own feet on the hard dry bed of the wadi, and our own horses trembled and quivered as we watched with envy the advance of those Light Horsemen. They spread across the plain like running water, roaring like Vikings, and there wasn't a man or a horse among us Yeomen that didn't then feel cheated not to be up there with them.

My mare snorted and trembled. She raised and lowered her head, snorting whimpering, every muscle quivering and twitching. Streaks of sweat marked the lines of her sinews and congealed down her forelegs.

'Unheard of,' the Lieutenant was saying. 'Cavalry against machine guns and artillery . . .'

We were all open-mouthed; we all were – those Australians went so fast, Jacko couldn't adjust his guns in time, and the Australians were galloping right in under the range of them and roaring and singing as they went.

They took Beersheba, the Australians, using the

rifle and bayonet as a lance, and we Yeomen had played no part in it at all.

In the purple dusk there was a great rumbling of wheels and hoofs as brigades and batteries raced to the town. The horses smelt the sweet scent of water across the dusty air and whinnied. An officer on horseback went out behind the men of the Light Horse, and there was the sound of pistol shots to the wounded horses that lay out there. When we crossed the Turk trenches, Ballard and Hadley and everyone stopped to sit down and eat jam and biscuit but I pushed on trying to find Captain and Hey-Ho.

I passed transport wagons, crumpled motor lorries, oxen, camels and mules, some dead, some moaning from their wounds, past all the jumbled wreckage of an army, the bits of wheel and wagon, bits of bullock, mules still yoked, one dead and fallen, the other on his knees, the sight enough to make you never want to see a war again. I thought of Mother and what she'd said about the way the Arabs looked after their animals.

The streets of Beersheba clattered as brigade after brigade filed in, ungirthed and unbridled, to let the horses drink from the wells. It was a miserable place, Beersheba, all brown earth hovels and choking heat, and a confusion of armoured cars, stinking camels, military police and transport dashing about with mounds of fodder, aeroplanes flying low, and cavalry details going from one place to another, and I was rounded up before I found Captain and made to push on.

After Beersheba, we Yeomen swept on, right up Palestine. In a front that ran from the coast to the hills, we chased the Turk all the way to Jaffa. The kitchens and Service Corps didn't keep up with us, and where Captain and Hey-Ho were, for a long time I didn't know.

Judaea

November 1917

We moved fast, were pushed then to the extremes of our strength, eating and sleeping as we could. I was apart for a long while from Captain. By November, we were in the Judaean foothills and we were in a terrible state, men and horses – no rations or water had reached us and we were suffering, all of us, from fatigue and burning thirst.

We'd got to some miserable place – Khulweife, it may have been – and were held up there for a while. The pack-animals were on their way up and Captain would be with them but before they arrived a troop of us cavalry were sent out along some valley or other. We were stuck there in that valley, waiting for an order to attack. Midday came with its scorching heat, every stone throwing the sun back at us. I tore the buttons from my tunic to suck on – I'd lost the pebble Captain had given me. We were in an agony of thirst, all of us. At sundown, we were still waiting and men were going delirious. For the thousandth time that day I looked to the head of the valley for the pack-animals, for the water and the kitchens. Night came and there was still no relief.

By dawn, we were wild and desperate and when Johnny Turk came, we had our guns on him. He came at us like a dervish, darting and dashing from the rocks, but we broke him and hurled him back.

Every fight was a fight for water. Either we drove the enemy away from it, or we had to go back to where we started, only to have to do it all again another day.

In respect of the water, at least, Huj was the same thing all over again. You see, Huj was the Worcestershire Yeomen's battle, and for once it wasn't the Australians who took the thunder: it was us. I think it was because of Huj and the glory of that day that things shifted again between Captain and me.

We looked like hooligans: hollow-eyed with hunger, unshaven – I was a bit proud of my chin just then, and could show it off, there being no shaving allowed, to save water.

We'd reached the place where Jacko had bivouacked the night before – he'd left kit and blankets and limber and fodder and all sorts lying around. It was Merriman who found the water barrels, but Jacko had left some rotting camel in them just for us and none of us drank from them.

Jacko had set himself up on a ridge. Southward he had a clear field of fire, but to his left, where the ridge curled to the right, there was a slight spur that ran down towards a wadi. We Yeomen were to creep along that wadi, one-and-a-half squadrons of us, and snake along its hidden folds. We moved fast, overtaking the Gloucester Yeomanry, the Sixtieth, the Light Horse, and all the other sorts that were there. We got ourselves ahead of the guns too, somehow, so when we reached a place where we were hidden from the enemy batteries, we dismounted to give our horses a breather.

There were Londoners to our left and they were having a hard time.

'Jacko's having it all his own way today,' said Ballard.

An officer came galloping up and spoke to the Major.

'Prepare to mount,' the Major barked. 'Form column of half-squadrons, draw swords.'

Now, looking back, I think that every man is scared before a battle, that you never lose your fear, however many times you go in; but in a mounted charge it's the courage of the whole and the excitement of your horse that sweeps you up in a drum roll of hoof and blood and muscle that pushes out your fear.

We moved off at a smart trot, rising and falling as one, knee to knee, as if on a drill ground, swords balanced across our thighs, tails flying. Jacko knew we were coming from the storm of dust we raised.

The horses sensed our excitement and fear. They

tossed and snorted and fidgeted, and my mare jostled Ballard's, every muscle in her taut, her neck streaked with sweat.

Jacko was ready for us, and opened fire the second we broached the ridge.

The order to charge was sounded.

It was like riding into hell. Jacko had shortened his fuses, his shrapnel bursting in our midst, but we never checked our speed and went yelling and roaring and riding straight at him with swords at the engage, the breath of his shells on our skin. I've never ridden harder or faster than at Huj. It was the open slope and the thrill of the pack – the thundering hoofs, the steaming flanks, the flying froth, the flaming nostrils, the straining muscle and the pounding of air and wind and sky – there was surely never anything like that charge at Huj in all history.

We flooded across the plain through screaming shells and whistling bullets. On either side horses blundered and fell. The line thinned as men fell from saddles, then suddenly Ballard was laughing and yelling and everyone was laughing and picking up still more speed – the shells were falling behind us and we were all roaring for joy that Jacko couldn't lower his guns in time to keep pace with the Worcester Yeomanry.

Jacko's gunners were setting the fuses at zero – firing point-blank – and we were in the gaping mouths of their guns, the muzzles flashing. I glimpsed a horse on his knees, a Sergeant slumped in the saddle, more horses going down. Over the rim of a trench, through the dust and confusion and tongues of flame, I saw a Turk abandon his gun, more of them turning and running.

The flash of our swords, the thunder of hoofs and the pace of our gallop terrified those Turks, and I don't think they'll ever hang around and wait for the charge of the Worcestershire Yeomanry again. Sweat ran in rivers down the horses' flanks, splattering into the dust, their nostrils wide and pulsing.

Oh, it was a glorious charge all right, the kind of charge of which every boy dreams, a day to make all the cavalry in France and Belgium weak with envy – the big, fast, open riding that was in our minds when we'd stood around Abel Rudge's desk. As I spurred my mare on, I thought, *God help me*, of Abel, hoping he'd read about us in the papers.

Jacko's men were running from cover to cover now, abandoning their positions, Yeomen leaping to the ground, fighting hand to hand, riderless horses racing along the parapet of the first trench, frothing and sweating, spume flying from their muzzles. Roaring and shouting, we burst through the battery position, riding down any of Jacko's men still manning a gun. Just a handful of Yeomen we were there, up at the first trench, and I was up beside the Lieutenant, and his arm was out and level, motioning us on to the rifle pits. With desperate bravado, Sparrow and Hadley leaped those trenches – and I followed – great plunging leaps over those guns – and there's nothing like the feel of flying over Jacko and his guns anywhere, even in the Grand National.

We were over the second rifle pit when I screamed – my mare landed badly, stumbling, a foreleg buckling. She went down with a sickening lurch, both forelegs doubled to the ground, and I was catapulted over her neck.

When I came to there was white linen over and under me, a line of cots stretching out on either side. I flexed each leg, then each arm, and ran a hand over each limb. No matter how many times you go up to fight, after every battle you're surprised to find yourself still alive. Every time.

Two days passed before the throbbing in my head stopped and I could focus my eyes. The sign on my table read:

SEVERE CONCUSSION

An orderly came to take my pulse, and check and measure all the usual things, then sat beside me and wrote some notes on a clipboard. He put down his pen and went to fetch some water. I was feeling fine so I picked up the pen.

'MILD,' I wrote, crossing out the 'SEVERE'.

'Does anyone know I'm here?' I asked.

'He comes every day, your friend Captain. 'He watches and he waits . . . every day.'

'Has anyone else come?' I asked.

'No . . . no one else. But your friend said to tell you your horse is just fine, that she got up and went on without you and charged all the way to Huj.'

The Major – Straker was promoted – after Huj – came to see me. Sparrow was now a full Lieutenant.

'Lance-Corporal Bayliss,' said Major Straker. 'Congratulations.'

Lance-Corporal.

I was rather pleased even though I knew we'd lost so many men at Huj that there were promotions being handed out all around the place.

The Major told me we'd had a message from the Commander-in-Chief, that we'd 'upheld the best traditions of the British cavalry', that 'for sheer bravery there'd been nothing ever like it'.

Ballard and Firkins came later, too. A parcel post had caught up with us there at Huj, a lot of mail all in one go. Firkins had a bag of goodies from home and we had a jolly time, all sitting round my bed, with cake and cigarettes and all kinds of luxuries, and we talked of Hadley and of Farmer, both of whom had fallen, and drank to ourselves, to the talk of all Palestine. It was different after Huj – or I was foolish enough to think it was different. You see, from that visit onwards I didn't feel like little Billy Bayliss– they didn't treat me like little Billy Bayliss any more. I was so buoyed up they'd come to see me and share their parcels with me that I never asked how Captain was.

When Lieutenant Sparrow came, he took the sign off the bed next door:

FIT FOR SERVICE

and swapped it with mine. Then he added a few words, so that it read:

THE LANCE CORPORAL IS *FIT FOR SERVICE*

'We need you, Billy,' he said.

There was to be a race meeting, with relays and all sorts, and to put on a good show, the Yeomen needed me to be fit and ready.

Chips came to see me later, and I thought he'd be proud of me, too, like the others seemed to be.

'Lance-Corporal Bayliss,' I told him proudly. I told him about the charge, the speed of it and the thrill of it, the leaping of the Turkish trenches. I was carried away by the glory of it all, and never noticed Chips's irritation until his jaws took the unusual step of stopping their chewing in preparation for what was, for Chips, a great peroration.

'He never stopped looking till he found that 'orse o' yours. That boy queued with her all night, from dark to dawn he and his donkey stood with 'er in a line that went from here to kingdom come, all night they waited for her turn to water. Not that you asked.'

PART IV

PALESTINE

After Huj

November 1917

After Huj, the Generals gathered the largest convention
of camels of all the centuries. They were everywhere –
garlands of the rudimentary creatures around every
telegraph pole – trains of the absurd, splay-foot animals
along every horizon. Fifty thousand of them were
purchased for the Cavalry and Transport; the stink of
them was everywhere, and you could have heard their
roaring for miles around. I'd put money on it never,
ever occurring to Abel Rudge that I'd end up riding
into battle on one of the brutes. No horseman has
much liking for a camel and we Yeomen had laughed
at the slobbering and the stink of them, and their
kicking and gurgling. Firkins said that a camel is made
up out of all the left over bits of all the other animals;
the head of a sheep on the neck of a giraffe on the
body of a cow and stuck on at the kicking end the tail
of a donkey; that their necks were bent in shame at
the way they'd been put together like that for a joke at
the end of the day and at the way they'd been sent to

live in the desert where no other animal can live and we'd all laughed at that; laughed until just then, after Huj, we were suddenly separated from our horses and transferred to the 'Camelry'. For the great Race Meeting we were to ride bits of all the other animals loosely held together instead of fine Yeomanry horses and we were all very put out about that.

My mare was noble, and fast, too, but I never deserved her because I was always longing for Trumpet's strength, for the chunkiness of him and his reassuring bulk. It was good, though, to think that she would have a break from the sand and blistering stones and thirst, because a horse isn't made the right way for that sort of country. The Generals knew that, and they were all in favour of the humpy-backed camels just then, because they could go so long without water.

They had a strong preference for bull camels, but in the train that came for us there was one cow camel, a great cream-coloured Amazonian with the usual rickety camel legs and a roar like the Day of Judgement. The very first thing she did was to give Firkins a well-aimed kick of a monstrous hind leg just when Firkins was at the height of a long speechification about the prominence of the camel in Genesis and Zechariah and all the other books of the Old Testament. Firkins might know a lot about the genesis of a camel but he didn't know that they can kick with all four of their legs and in all directions. I was laughing the most when Firkins was doubled up in the dust with his pipe spinning down after him, so he squeaked out, 'Let young Billy have her then.'

At this moment the beast began to put her lips together and pout in an ominous sort of way. I didn't know then what the pursing of the lips of a camel means, but I can tell you now that it portends the dredging up from the very nethermost corner of a camel's digestion an indescribable blend of fermented spittle and cud that it intends to spout with all the considerable force it can muster in your direction. She hadn't liked me laughing and wanted to show me a thing or two, I think, and decided to aim that mouthful at me. So I was standing there, feeling foolish, not laughing at all and dripping with camel spit, and the men were all laughing like drains. I was laughing too. The only one who wasn't laughing just then was the camel because a camel takes itself very seriously.

Firkins was laughing the most, at this moment, and it was him who said again, 'Give the sweet little dolly to young Billy. She likes him.'

Firkins was feeling sour, I think, about the kick he'd had, but then Skerret said, 'Dolly. Give him Dolly.' And then they were all still laughing like drains and chanting, 'Dolly!'

Dolly. The name stuck straight away, being so comical when you took into account the height of her being that of a house. 'Dolly, give him Dolly!' – while I was still wiping the noxious stuff from my face.

I was popular just then with all the men after the success at Huj, you see, and they liked to tease me, but I was easier with their teasing now, didn't mind it in the way I had when I felt it was because I was so young and they were mocking me. You see, I'd been out there longer than most of them, and the way they treated me after Huj was very different. They teased me, but I'd been at Gallipoli and Gaza, and I knew my way about.

'Billy, she has good blood. A racing camel,' Captain told me later, and it was true that she wasn't at all in the ordinary run of Indian brown camels the other men had. But Dolly thought, me, from the start, far, far beneath her dignity. Chewing casually, she looked over my head and allowed her slaver to trickle carelessly from her rudimentary jaws down her many sagging chins. I approached her with an attempt at an open mind, smiling and sort of cooing at her, and in turn she bared her yellow fangs at me. Those jaws towered a full three foot over the crown of my head, and I stepped back in horror at them and at the slobber and stink of her. Captain laughed at me and I pulled a face. Dolly displayed her towering indifference to us all by continuing to chew and slaver right there over the top of me. She had a throat like one of the older drainpipes at Bredicot – a great burbling and gurgling going on at all hours, as if all the rivers of Worcestershire were inside it.

'A well-bred camel,' Major Straker told me, 'has a gait so smooth you can drink a cup of coffee on it at a gallop.'

Well, you have to get on a camel before you can test that theory, and in order to get on it, you have to get the preposterous-looking creature to kneel. So there we all were on that first Mounted Drill saying 'Duh-duh-duh', because an Egyptian camel knows by 'Duh-duh-duh' that it must *barak*, or kneel. I twitched at Dolly's nose rope to encourage her to *barak*, but a good horseman never likes to pull too hard at a rein, especially if that rope is pierced through the nostril, so I did it a little gingerly. Dolly curled her lips and snarled and displayed a disquieting array of yellow-green gnashers. She smacked her lips and she bared those gnashers again and indicated, very clearly, that she had no intention whatsoever of kneeling or indeed of doing my bidding at any time. So now I pulled at the rope and at this she raised her lids a fraction and appeared to consent to give the idea of kneeling her consideration. I pulled again and again but she went about such a lengthy consideration of my request that I began to forget about the matter of kneeling and was beginning to think instead about what there might be for lunch, when suddenly she decided that she did, after all, want to kneel. And she did this in such a way – lifting her head and lowering her lids – as to make it quite clear that her deciding to kneel had no connection whatsoever with my asking her to do so.

There is some majesty to the movement of a camel, and Dolly, being a most stately and leisurely sort of camel, was a great upholder of this general truth. Looking as though her thoughts were centred entirely on the most lofty and elevated of matters and not remotely on the business of what her legs were doing, she began to sink and double the lowest section of her forelegs, then to lower and fold the lower part of her hind legs. Then she embarked on the bending of the upper bones of her forelegs over the lower bones of them and on the settling of the lower bones of her hind legs over all the other bits, and all this was going with tremendous groaning and grunting, until finally every scabby, knobbly joint was bent and every section of every rickety limb was in a new position and folded up and arranged – almost – to her satisfaction. At this point, her very considerable belly subsided, much in the manner of the slow collapsing of a marquee, and engulfed the whole new configuration of herself. But even then she wasn't finished, because she gave a terrific moan about the palaver of it all and then began quite a new rearrangement of all the various sections of herself.

By then I was wondering why out of every animal that came from the ark I had been given this finicky, fractious creature, and was growing a little concerned too about the likelihood of her ever standing up again and staying in one piece for even the smallest length of time, because having seen what a profligate number of bits and pieces there are to the limb of a camel, I had begun to wonder how it ever stays together at all or moves anywhere without all falling to pieces.

Every day that I had Dolly, she would observe this joint-by-rickety-joint ritual with strict protocol and there was nothing doing, ever, to hurry her.

'Prepare to mount.'

At this stage in the game you are supposed to pull the camel's head round and position a foot on the curve of its neck. Now, Dolly's response to the placing of a foot on her neck was to bare her teeth in a most villainous sort of way, as if to dare me to so much as dream of mounting, and then to smack her lips and pout. I saw that pout and knew what it portended and decided I was safer on her than off, so, fairly fast, I threw my right leg over the front peg of the saddle.

We were instructed to rise, so I gave the command we'd been told was appropriate in the circumstances.

'Goom! Goom!' I commanded.

At 'goom-goom', any reasonable camel will stand up. Dolly, however, put her lids at half-mast again and raised her nose and set about staring with cast-iron malice into the middle distance. I loosened her rein and goom-goomed her again but she was particularly set on staying down. Every one of us Yeomen was goom-gooming and every one of those crabby, contrary creatures was looking elsewhere and chewing the cud as if there were no such thing at all as a Yeoman of Worcestershire on its back, and making every one of us just long for a plain old, good old horse. Then one or two of the creatures stopped their slavering and began to grunt and groan and to hoist themselves up. If a camel has to get to its feet, it likes to roar while it's about it, and the roar of that whole line of camels that was hoisting itself to its feet in Palestine was a sound that might have been heard in Paris.

Dolly chewed and I goom-goomed and goom-goomed, and she chewed some more, and I tapped her on the nose, and tapped her on the nose again, and so on till suddenly I leaped with fright at the roar that erupted from the depths of her. Like the crack of doom it was. She lurched me back and pitched me forward, and it was like being hurled over the crest of a tsunami on a raft, and all the while she bellowed so broadly she could surely be heard in Damascus.

A camel's saddle has no stirrups to it, so I gripped the handle of the saddle, but nothing in all my Old Testament reading had prepared me for the way the unfolding of a camel can throw you forward till you feel your teeth'll hit the ground; because a camel is so peverse a creature as to like to stand hind legs first.

There I was, up there in the stratosphere, realizing

that you need a good head for heights to sit on a camel like her. Skerret and Ballard were laughing at me, and Captain was laughing at all of us, so I gripped my peg and hooked my shaking legs around the cantles of the wooden saddle, and I tried to forget that my head was almost at the telegraph wires.

I tried to muster some authority over her. I tap-tapped her on the neck. Dolly took one mincing step, lifted her head and stepped forward in a mighty unpredictable sort of way, as though she were walking over hot coals. I could still hear Ballard laughing so I tapped again, and Dolly decided to take up this raking stride, which is not in the reasonable way of a horse at all. I am almost certain that there are both spite and malice in the gait of a camel, both right legs going forward, then both left legs, much in the way of an elephant and, deliberately it seemed to me, so as to pitch the rider from side to side.

We mucked about like schoolboys, while they bellowed and slavered, leaped about like kangaroos and shied or swerved with shock at the slightest sound or flutter of a palm frond.

Later Captain found me trying to hobble Dolly in the lines.

'She's a good camel, Billy,' he said.

He ran his hand along the swayed curve of her neck, tugged on her nose rope till her eyes were level with his, and blew into her terrifying nose holes in the way

Liza liked to do with Trumpet. The hoods of Dolly's eyes sank with all the majesty of the crimson curtain at the end of a great London show, and I was a little irritated at that, and annoyed with myself because I was still fumbling with the rope.

'White coat means pure blood, very special.'

'She certainly thinks she's rather special,' I replied tautly, because I took a rather dim view of her still.

Captain had some dates in his pocket and it was maybe because of those dates that Dolly took to him and to Hey-Ho. In her mind, he and Hey-Ho and dates all came together, and she immediately formed the unshakeable opinion that they were a good trio to come your way.

Later – another night, perhaps – Captain ran his hand beneath her belly, slow and searching, then did the same again, a little higher up, running it from foreleg to the hind leg, frowning a little.

'A cow camel is quiet and good,' he said then, and he gave me some dates for her, still eyeing her in a quizzical sort of way.

I held out my palm while Dolly gave a good impression of not knowing I was there at all, even as she golloped the dates in my hand.

'Cow camels better, faster . . .'

'We'll see.'

'. . . Because they have to run away.'

The idea of Dolly in flight at top gear from a thing

she feared was something I didn't much fancy, and I was quiet while I thought about it.

'All racing camels are cows. Very important you move slowly round her. Always,' Captain said.

Dolly had a great many dislikes and seemed to bear a grudge against most living things, most especially horses. Horses too had a great dislike for her, as they do for all camels. If a horse happened by, Dolly might flick and lash her scraggy tail about or, if her greed, malice and humour were all uppermost in her heart at the same time, she'd eat through her ropes and wander off to cause trouble in the horse lines just for the fun of it. But to Dolly, Hey-Ho was a different case: she tolerated Hey-Ho as she tolerated no other animal.

After the first long trek Dolly and Hey-Ho made together, a surprising thing happened. Captain and I were cooking when we heard a great shouting and commotion in the mule lines. The syces and the Catering Corps and the Transport Corps people were all flapping their arms, and the mules were all shrieking, so we went to see what was going on – and there, stampeding up and down the lines and bellowing, was Dolly. She found Hey-Ho, and stopped, and nosed her way in beside him. Looking more preposterous than ever there, with the mules all around her knees, she grew still and quiet. Hey-

Ho was at her side and her haughty lids gentled and dropped. Nothing perturbed little Hey-Ho – nothing except the absence of Captain – and, so long as Captain was close by, Hey-Ho accepted all manner of things; even a camel in his bed-quarters. They became like mother and son to each other. They made strange companions, the pair of them, tethered side by side, each as ancient and biblical as the other, the stoical and stout-hearted donkey, and the savage, supercilious camel.

I'd like to say I loved Dolly, though I never did. She towered over all other camels, standing as she did a full twenty-four hands to her withers, and was, in her way, as stately and splendid as a cathedral. She bore herself like a monarch, as though she had no notion at all that her back was humped or her knees knocking or legs just rickety spindles. If you consider the prodigality of her construction, she had a surprising and decidedly delicate disposition and was liable to a vast number of complaints and ailments. This delicacy in her constitution was surprising, given her ability to digest all manner of things without doing herself a mischief: boxes of matches, saddles, ropes, halters, blankets, kitbags, prickly pears – I swear she'd eat tombstone if it were to hand. The great spectrum of things Dolly was *not* above eating was a source of delight to Captain, and he, I think, did love her – for many things, but most especially for the intricacy and the absurdity of her construction, for the comedy of her gurgling and spitting and slathering, and also because she'd taken so to Hey-Ho.

It was Captain who showed me that I had to treat her as gently, and with as much respect, as a horse, and when I put my face to her gaping nose holes, each the size of a Bredicot dinner plate, and blew, she now made it clear that this met with her approval, her lids closing in a decidedly contented way; and this went on for perhaps a bit too long, because she got into her head to relax completely and to *barak*, starting to go through her entire collapsing operation, and Captain was laughing at both of us. His laughter always came so readily, and at simple things.

'She is fast,' Captain said.

Later, when I went to my tent, Ballard and the others were talking about the Sports Meeting and camel races and how the Yeomen would turn out fit for a King's Parade. The next day we were all training like mad, and spitting and polishing till there was no more spit or polish to be had anywhere. I grew serious about those races, very serious. I was a Lance-Corporal, I had a tall, cream-coloured racing camel who put my head in the stratosphere, and everyone was counting on me.

I stroked and groomed Dolly and I blew into her nose at all hours, and fed her dates, but I worried that there was something wrong when her hair came out in my hands after every stroke of my brush. I thought of Liza's letter about the Gyppos, and got it into my head then that Dolly had been mistreated or starved and needed feeding up. She had extravagance and spirit, but she'd had a hard time of it, and I decided I must get her into condition and stop her hair falling out, and put on a good show – because Ballard and the Major and everyone had money on her.

'Dolly needs more food,' I told Captain.

He shook his head, smiling mysteriously. Hey-Ho was close by, one ear dropping, the other upright. He brayed, and brushed his tail from side to side against the flies. Dolly grunted at him.

'She needs hard food.'

Captain shook his head.

'I'm going to feed her up,' I said.

I could see Ballard and the men setting up jumps of sandbag and scrub, others marking starting lines and fencing show-rings. Captain's eyes were on my hands as he asked, 'What with? Where from?'

Lieutenant Sparrow and some subalterns were marking out the course, and Major Straker was setting up a starting board. I wandered away towards the betting enclosure to have a closer look at it all. I saw how big the whole thing would be, with the stands and all the chairs being set up, then I turned around to Captain and said, 'If you won't help me, I'll get it on my own.'

We went together, he and I, but it was me who took the extra corn, it was me who went in and got it.

After the first heats Dolly was one of the favourites. There was hot competition – seven other good camels – but now all the Yeomanry pinned their hopes on her. They'd been glorious, the trials, at sunset, and I'd put her through her best paces and she'd gone like a dream, smooth as silk. I was showing off and I drank a *café au lait* on her at a gallop, like Major Straker said you could, and everyone was cheering. In the canteen that evening, after the heats, Ballard and Firkins were huddled, studying the form.

'I've money on Dolly, an advance on my daybook for you,' Firkins told me, and it turned out that everyone was having a flutter – Carter and Ballard, even the Major and the Lieutenant – and then they were all arguing among themselves about how best to ride bareback on a camel, whether I should be astride Dolly's hump or on her rump. I was already thinking about getting more corn for Dolly and how I might borrow Hey-Ho, because a sack of corn big enough for a camel is too heavy for a man to carry on his own.

When it came to it, there were benches to sit on and ladies with white dresses and transport wagons decked out in regimental colours and Generals and shining motors, and I wished Liza and Mother could've been there to see me on Dolly, so high up with my head at the telegraph wires. That Sports Meeting was within only a few miles of Jacko and all his army, but you'd never have known it for the amount of beer and bunting and lemonade and parasols that day. All the races were oversubscribed, and no admission was to be charged for entry, so the ground was bursting at the seams with animals and men and onlookers.

Like every other entrant, I thought my mount was the fastest. I was rather full of myself, what with all the Yeomen putting money on me and wanting me to ride for them; proud, too, to think that Dolly and I were part of the largest body of mounted troops the modern world had ever known; proud that I carried a rifle and a sword; proud to ride a cream-coloured racing camel. I felt that nothing could touch me – that I'd been at Gallipoli and Gaza and Huj – and before Major Straker came to me, I thought I could do as I please, go wherever the fighting was worst and come out untouched.

'Bayliss.' The Major pulled me aside.

'You're up for it, Lance-Corporal. The Quarter-master's got it in for you.'

Just then Dolly began to mince and jiggle, and I was thinking more about the difficulty of getting her to the start line, and trying to catch the voice on the loudspeaker, than about what Major Straker was saying.

'. . . *and the prize for the Best Turnout goes to the Bing*

Boys . . . *Ladies and gentlemen, make your way to the second track where the High Jump is about to commence . . .*'

'It's serious, Bayliss.'

'Sir, no, sir.' Then I laughed and looked away and tugged uselessly at Dolly's rope.

Dolly minced and jigged a bit more, and I busied myself with tapping her and patting her, all of which makes no difference to a camel's state of mind at all.

'Bayliss – you were seen . . .'

I looked away.

'Billy, Billy. For God's sake, Billy, I hope . . .'

Firkins and Archie Pimm were walking past just then.

'Bring back the pennant for the Yeomen, Billy,' said Archie Pimm.

'*The Border Stakes, for ponies fourteen-three or under, open to all ranks of the Desert Column . . .*'

'You won't even see us,' I answered Pimm, 'we'll be going so fast.' My voice sounded false, even to myself.

The Major looked at me with a thoughtful expression, then said, 'Billy, do you know anything about that corn?'

A starter was trying to marshal thirty unwilling mules up to a post with no gate.

'No sir.'

'The QM says Captain was there two nights ago. He saw two figures there at the door. When he checked, there was a sack of corn missing.' My stomach turned.

'Billy, he knows Captain was there, because there was a donkey outside, but he is certain he actually saw you there too.'

I was only half listening, my mind on the race ahead.

He stepped closer. 'It's serious, Billy,' he hissed. 'It's a serious offence. There's First Field Punishment for this kind of thing . . .'

My legs turned to water at this. First Field Punishment is a terrible thing – they can put you on a wheel for a day – and while I was thinking about that, the Major put a warning hand on my elbow.

'He's here,' he said. 'He's coming this way.'

The QM's face was as puffy as a quilt, even though the morning was still fresh. We all knew he was a drinker, best avoided in the mornings.

'Corporal Bayliss.'

'Sir.'

He was fondling the handle of his revolver.

'You were seen near the stores.'

'Sir . . . there's a mistake,' I said hesitantly.

'There's no mistake, Corporal. You were seen.'

I was silent.

'You'll come with me, Bayliss.'

Dolly snarled and bared her teeth, not liking the look of the QM, probably.

The Major stepped in then, and said, 'Quartermaster, see him afterwards, will you? He's on, next race, going to bring back the pennant for the Yeomen.' He had a commanding way about him always, did Major Straker, and what with that, together with Dolly's bare gnashers, and a Major being so senior to a Quartermaster in the pecking order of things, the QM was beginning to feel a little uncomfortable.

Then Captain was there, from nowhere, stepping forward.

'It *is* a mistake, sir,' Captain said, very calmly. 'It was me who went into the stores, sir.'

'Billy . . . ?' hissed Straker.

I bowed my head.

'It was me, sir,' Captain repeated.

I felt queasy with guilt and relief, but I thought perhaps it wouldn't matter so much if you took the blame when you weren't a Lance-Corporal and you weren't in the regular Army.

'*Entrants for the Promised Land Stakes, please come now to the paddock . . .*'

'Billy . . . ?' Major Straker whispered again.

Perhaps the QM was mistaken. Perhaps Captain had taken corn, too, for Hey-Ho; perhaps the QM had seen him, and not me. All sorts of desperate low excuses were running through my head just then.

The QM's eyes left me reluctantly, as if deprived of his prize, and turned to Captain, who stood there opposite us, with Hey-Ho at his side.

'*We have Horace, Strychnine and Starlight in the*

paddock, the brown Bikaner camel is Horace, and following Horace is . . .'

I was about to protest, about to step forward, but Captain met my eyes and moved his head from side to side, and I knew what he meant: *Say nothing, let me take the rap.*

'Billy?' hissed Straker again. 'Billy, you can't . . .'

I said nothing.

The Major took Captain by the arm and turned to the QM.

'Quartermaster, he's one of mine, and I'll be dealing with him myself.'

'Sir, as you like, sir.' The QM looked at me then; strangely, because he knew it was me who had been seen in the stores.

'You wait here,' the Major said.

'Yes, sir,' answered Captain.

What sort of punishment would the Major give Captain? I raised my eyes to his, praying he would be gentle. He looked at me, his face still troubled.

'All right, Bayliss . . .' With a conscious effort he lightened his tone and clapped me on the back. 'We're counting on you. Hurry, you've only a minute or so.'

As I mounted Dolly, I saw Straker order Captain off and hoped that he'd just be given some minor fatigue or other. Straker smiled grimly to himself, then turned to the ring. Captain was walking in the direction of the latrines and mess tent.

Sick with shame and guilt, I guided Dolly towards the paddock. Everywhere men shouted out to me, and waved, and admired Dolly's creamy coat and great height and swaying walk.

'Don't let us down!' Worcestershires were calling out from everywhere. I regretted, too, that Captain wouldn't see the race.

'Tom Thumb and Mahogany are entering the paddock . . .'

I saw the bookies' stands: Dolly was chalked up there with our odds: neck and neck as the favourite with Mahogany, who belonged to a General.

All of us somehow got our mounts to the start line, and *baraked* in a disorderly fashion, each of us pointing in different directions, as though on our own particular course to some far-flung corner of the world. I was the only one facing forward, and I was beginning to think I'd win because my racing camel clearly knew what all this was about.

The whistle blew.

Dolly rose up in her usual alarming sort of way, but I was still on her, and it was all going well when she suddenly spun round. I was still more or less astride her, but feeling things were going rather less well when she plumped herself firmly down in the reverse direction.

'They've got away to a good start – all except Lance-Corporal Bayliss there at the back, on Dolly . . .'

I thought of Major Straker and Lieutenant Sparrow, and all the money that was on me, and all the pride of the regiment . . . and I got red and hot with the shame of facing the wrong way round, there on the ground, with Dolly frothing casually and looking into the middle distance and considering what to do with the afternoon while I tapped and goom-goomed and tap-tapped, and she pretended to have no knowledge at all of what I wanted her to do.

'There're two unknowns at the back there: Tom Thumb and Gaza – and Gaza's coming up in a great rush . . . and at the back there, Dolly, still chewing the cud and contemplating the horizon . . .'

I heard the laughter of the crowd, and grew hotter, and tapped her harder. Then Dolly decided – and it had nothing, of course, to do with my tapping her – that our interests lay in the same direction. She rose with a violent malevolence and pitched me forward.

'The unknown in fourth place is bounding off like a kangaroo, and his rider's more off than on – will he hang on there or won't he? – No – he's off, but Cromwell's off the track – heading south – and Corporal Gene's mount – Horace, today ridden by his adjutant – is galloping like a champion, ahead of the favourite, Mahogany, and Starlight's not far behind . . .'

From half sitting, Dolly sprang away. There were roars of applause and laughter as I grabbed tufts of her hair, trying to balance myself and regain some composure.

'They say it's impossible to predict the winner of a camel scurry, and this morning it looks very much as though it is . . . Major Buxton's Waterloo is showing us a clean pair of heels, he's far ahead, going like a champion, but Starlight's on the way, catching up, a length ahead – but no! Something's upset poor Starlight – a parasol perhaps – she's zig-zagging off – she's broken the cordon . . . Watch out, everyone, Starlight's going for the tea tent . . .'

People were rushing out of the tea tent in alarm, spilling out of it from all sides.

'Yes, Starlight's still going . . . she's taking Colonel Langley off to get a cream tea – No – she's changed her mind, it's not a cream tea she's after . . . she's heading for Damascus! We won't be seeing Colonel Langley for some time – he and Starlight are off to take Damascus single-handed . . .'

There was a great roar from the crowd at this.

'At the back there – Lance-Corporal Bayliss is pointing the right way now, and Dolly is off, and she's got a good reach to her leg, it's long and low and . . .'

I tapped Dolly on, mercilessly; burning with shame I was, and venting it all on her. Hatless and saddle-less, heels tucked in tight, I tapped her again and again, though I no longer cared about the money that was on her, nor about the pride of the regiment. In her own good time she put on the spurt of speed I knew was in her – but suddenly, as though the idea of a race had just occurred to her, and that she had developed a sudden longing to get to the finish line.

The crowd was cheering and yelling, but I was nauseous still with guilt. Major Straker had defended Captain and I hadn't. What sort of friend *was* I? Major Straker had seen my cowardly performance there, in front of the QM. He knew I hadn't been truthful and that I'd let poor Captain take the rap.

I tucked my heels in, feeling another spurt of speed and enjoying it, the extravagance of it fitting the recklessness I felt, the anger at myself.

'*Tom Thumb's heading for Cairo, for Constantinople, Aleppo, he might go anywhere – he's going everywhere but straight down the line . . . but Lance-Corporal Bayliss and Dolly are catching up the head of the race, and that's from a sitting start, gentlemen . . .Tom Thumb's proving erratic in all the excitement . . . but he's back on track, and Dolly – she could even be bred for the track! – It'll be the Fourth Battalion taking home the pennant if she can overtake Strychnine . . . Oh, there's nothing like a camel scurry! Well, Tom Thumb there, we don't know what he's going to do next – hold on to your hats, everyone – Look! Dolly is on the final straight, she was only warming up until now and listen to the crowd – how it loves a plucky rider – The Lance-Corporal was at Gallipoli – at Gaza, at Beersheba, at Huj – Lance-Corporal Bayliss of the Worcestershire Yeomanry, of the Queen's Own Hussars – here on Dolly for the Promised Land Stakes – a race open to all ranks of the Desert Column – she's opening up like a winner – she's taken on another lease of life! – She's over the finish! – Dolly it is! – Dolly and Lance-Corporal Bayliss – over five furlongs, they've beaten the competition hands down – winners of the Promised Land Stakes!'*

I was carried shoulder-high through the crowd, born overhead by a thousand hands, but they were never Captain's and it was never his face I saw when I looked for it.

Somewhere there was bareback wrestling on camels. Somewhere else an egg-and-spoon race was going on, riders' faces comical with concentration, the camels greatly indifferent to it all. I led Dolly from place to place in search of Captain, and everywhere she was given grapes and cream cakes, and she slathered and slobbered in her customary way and indicated that she knew nothing about cheering crowds or any such thing as a race at all.

There was a concert and dancing and a prize giving. I stepped forward to receive the Cup and the pennant. The Worcestershire Yeomanry give the loudest hurrahs, so Ballard and all of them took the roof off the tent at that moment, but Major Straker never clapped me at all.

I left the tent and went out alone to where I was certain Captain would be. I would have given him the regimental silver if I could; would have said what I wanted to if I could find the words for it. But instead, when I found him there in the mule lines beside Hey-Ho, all I said was: 'This is for you. We brought this back, Dolly and I, we brought it back for you.' I showed him the rosette.

'Dolly won,' he said, and he broke into a wide smile and he hugged me.

As I pinned the gaudy rosette to Hey-Ho's halter I said, 'It's for you and for Hey-Ho.'

Hey-Ho tossed his head in protest at the fluttering tails of it on his cheek.

'He says he is very proud of you,' said Captain.

The rosette looked brash on Hey-Ho's wise, grave head. I looked down.

'I am not very proud of me,' I said.

Captain was silent, waiting.

'I'm sorry,' I said finally.

He smiled then, in a way that said that punishments and such things meant nothing to him, that our friendship meant something to him, that I and Hey-Ho were all that mattered.

'Anyway . . .' he said. 'You were right to want hard food for her.'

I looked up, puzzled, but all he would say in explanation was: 'Dolly has a secret.'

'What's that?'

You don't really want to be atop a camel that has

any kind of secret: they are dangerous enough, just as they are.

'She is not yet ready to share it with you,' Captain answered, and we were both laughing then at the notion of a camel having a secret that it has not yet decided to publicize.

You get all sorts of punishments if you're in the regular Army, even for silly offences. For almost nothing at all you can get tied to a wheel for an hour a day for fourteen days. Captain had done two hours' extra grooming, which was just a token punishment because the Major knew Captain had taken the rap for me.

I have the pennant here. I carried it with me all the way to Damascus. Nurse has ironed and hung it by my bed, unaware how pinching are the memories it brings.

Somewhere in the Desert

November 1917

Some time around then, just after the races, I was sent out with sixteen men, all of us under the command of Lieutenant Sparrow, from one sand hole to some other sand hole, the idea being to act as a guard to the flanks of the main artery of the army and to reconnoitre, to find out if the Turks were preparing to attack from the east. Captain was to come too, with Hey-Ho there being little work at the camp just then.

I wasn't amused by the way Dolly was jigging and jogging like a show pony, and looking about herself in a hoity-toity, displeased sort of way. She stopped suddenly, abruptly snatched her head to the ground to pull out, roots and all, some spiky stubble grass, and pitched me headlong down her serpentine neck. I scrabbled back up and more or less into position, then caught Captain grinning at us both with amusement. Dolly belched, and green slime poured over her yellow teeth and in and out of every fold of her several chins, and I was irked by the indignity of it, me being a Lance-Corporal and all.

We awoke, the second morning of that trek, to the scent of the sun-warmed wormwood, and my first thought was what sort of state of mind I might find Dolly in. You see, you never know which side of a bed a camel will choose to wake up on, and to be anywhere near a camel, especially Dolly, at breakfast time when she was always in a hump, can be a risky sort of business. She woke that particular morning snarling and roaring with astonishment and dismay at the sleeping conditions offered to her by the British Army. Firkins came out of his tent and didn't peg the opening down, so it was there, flapping in the wind, while Firkins set about lighting his pipe. Dolly took a great exception to the flapping of that tent. Tearing the rope from my hands, she went roaring and bellowing off in her unfathomable way towards some random point that she'd hit upon, that was no different to any other point in that blank empty country we were in.

'More human than a horse,' said Captain, grinning fondly as my mount disappeared.

'Inconsistent. Unpredictable. Like my wife,' said Firkins, laughing.

I wasn't laughing, though, because it is no joke losing a camel in a desert, and it was annoying that Firkins was laughing because it was his tent flap that sent Dolly running. She was daft as a brush, Dolly, really . . . She showed a proud indifference to all sorts of fire, but just the first squeak of a bagpipe, or the merest flap of a flag, and she'd fly off the handle and career away to the back end of beyond. On top of that, I was a bit surprised by Firkins having a wife at all, seeing as he'd never mentioned her and seeing as she'd have to live at close hand with his pipe and that history-spouting at all hours . . .

Dolly came to an abrupt halt, some spiny twig or other having taken her fancy to eat. I was relieved, because if she was scared she could outrun any horse, and sometimes I had to wait a good many hours till she decided to return. Hey-Ho, on the other hand, was always allowed to graze loose.

That morning I watched, sulking, as the little donkey wandered away, nibbling at the prickles he so loved and turning from time to time to see if Captain were coming or if he could hear his voice. When he turned to look for Captain, his good ear would be up, his eyes round and deep, and there was something so sincere in his searching for Captain that made me wish for some other animal than Dolly – some tender creature who'd search for me in the same way. At the end of the day, if we were in camp, when Hey-Ho heard the blowing of the Last Post, he'd lift his head from the thistles and plod straight away home, and park himself in his section of the line, bang in the right place. Hey-Ho submitted himself to the general good, took his master's goal to his own heart, while

Dolly could only be persuaded into doing a thing for me if it served her own purposes too.

'Here. Take these.' Captain slipped some dates into my pocket. 'Copy me,' he said, then patted his pocket and turned his back and whistled.

We walked on a few steps, whistling and patting our pockets. After a bit I sneaked a backwards glance.

'She's coming, Captain, she's coming,' I said, and I was mighty relieved, and amused too, because Dolly was heading our way while still managing to pretend that we and our dates were entirely beneath her consideration.

'Keep walking,' he said, grinning.

Then suddenly Dolly was there, right behind me, and lowering her great nose to my pocket. She found the dates, and slobbered and drooled from her lips while her eyes looked at the horizon, as if she could take or leave the dates and they were nothing to her at all. Captain tickled her behind the ears, and so did I, and then her lids were dropping, and almost closing, and she started up a sort of purring sound like a cat, and Captain and I were grinning over her ears at the preposterousness of a camel.

On the morning of the third day, we stopped to breakfast on small portions of salt bacon, hard biscuits and tea, each of us carrying four days' rations. The sandhills were steep and deep, like cliffs almost, and far higher than any hill in Worcestershire. The sun turned the sand red-hot and made the air shimmer. In the height of the day, our mouths turned raw from thirst, the sun hammering down on our heads with all the heat of a furnace and turning everything to mirage and illusion.

Hey-Ho was slow and floundering. He suffered more than the camels in the deep sand and on the sharp rocks. His eyes turned red from the sun and the flying sand. Dolly's head dropped too. The rocks cracked the soft pads of her feet and she flinched at every pebble as though it were a hot coal.

We struggled on without water, on and on, over the white-hot sand, under the white-hot sun, the waves of heat sinking and rising, eddying around and around, our lips growing cracked and shrunken, our rifles too hot to touch.

The deadliest enemy wasn't Jacko, you see: out there, it was always the desert sun.

The following day we headed homewards: back down the mountains, then on along the bed of a dry wadi. The night was bitter. We found some or other inhospitable crook or cranny to rest in, and drew lots for the order of sentry. We rolled up in our blankets in hollows of sand, rifles loaded in our hands, each of us facing out in a different direction.

Despite the general malevolence of Dolly, and her evil smell, I had taken to using her forelegs as a pillow, and they were serviceable enough for that. But the thing that really puts a spanner in the works when you're trying to kip beside a camel is the mountainous gurgling and bubbling that goes on all night in all four of its stomachs. On top of that, I was nervous of doing sentry duty. When the temperature dropped and I was soaked to the bone by dew, I gave up and paced up and down until it was time to relieve the Lieutenant. I was very serious just then about my duty there, as the nerve-end of the right flank of the British Army. Overtired and fraught, every sound was making me jump and start. The mesh of tangled thorn against the sky grew sinister. Soon, in my imagining, the whole of the night was menacing and every thorn and bush seemed thick with Jacko's men.

Some nightbird, or other thing, squawked. Then there was silence. I thought that the silence was strange, because no other bird had squawked back, and one bird always answers another. I wished someone were awake to keep me company. The scrub shadow moved again on the white sand, and I thought I caught the murmuring of a human voice, and perhaps the sound of metal on stone; and then I thought I was just going mad with imaginings till I heard what I was sure was a voice. I woke the Lieutenant, and he woke Firkins and sent him off to the main wadi to warn the next outpost. Archie Pimm and I were told to cover the ground in front and on the flank. The Lieutenant himself took up position at the point where the track crossed the bed of the tributary.

The silence was split with a crackle of fire from somewhere – spurts of red in the dark – and all of us answered with fire of our own. Jacko stopped his fire. There was silence for a while, and we all in our separate positions waited tensely. After a while, Lieutenant Sparrow crept up behind me and whispered, 'Bayliss, find out where they've gone. Follow if you can . . . and take care.'

I collected Dolly, who wasn't keen on this new project, nor on being taken away from Hey-Ho and the others. Truth be told, neither was I, but I mounted and set off fearfully into the moonless night, wishing Dolly's digestion was not quite so loud, because it was loud enough for every Jacko in every wadi of all Arabia to hear. I approached the point the Turkish fire had been coming from, and saw blankets and implements abandoned and, among them, with a sickening turn of the stomach, two bodies tangled in some undergrowth.

The rest had escaped, and it was my job to track them down. I steeled myself on. Dolly herself was going happily along the sand and pebble of that river bed, it being the old path home. It grew foggy. The stars were blotted out, and the dark felt thick and haunted, and you couldn't see very far ahead, not only because of the creeping fog, but also because of the rocks and boulders that lay tumbled about everywhere. We turned a crooked leg of the wadi and the footprints we'd been following disappeared.

I urged Dolly up the bank. I tapped her, she grunted and groaned and stood firm, and we had a fight to see which of us would get their own way. She belched, and then, in her own good time, took one picky, mincing step up, and then waited, and so on, and all the while she was curling her neck and stretching it out and developing a great longing to be with Hey-Ho and her fellow camels; and I realized that all this shilly-shallying was about her objection to this new direction not being homewards. Somehow or other, I got her to the top of the bank, and there, where the breeze felt fresh and cooling, I let her rest, and looked about with all my senses on edge.

There was a whistling, or some sound other than the wind. I saw something black ahead, a little way below, but in the fog I couldn't tell how far it was, nor what. I dismounted, my heart beating against my ribs like a moth trapped in a palm, and looped Dolly's head-stall round a tamarind tree.

The thing was moving softly, but had most definitely moved. I thought of the others asleep somewhere, or peacefully homeward bound, while I was here alone with Dolly, and Jacko right there in front of me, creeping like a mongoose straight towards the British camp.

I crept, rifle in hand and loaded down inch by

inch, so as to see around a rock that obstructed my view – to see how many men were down there. I prayed Dolly was happily eating that tamarind and that she wouldn't belch or bellow or roar. I crouched and waited and shivered and peered, but my eyes were tired and streaming.

There – twelve, sixteen, twenty Turks – further away, more still – a hundred or more – all of them huddled darkly like carrion birds.

I thought for a second about Dolly's leisurely *barak* routine, and decided I would mount her standing and race back to HQ to report what I'd seen. Inch by inch, tearing my skin on the prickles of the spiny things that grow in those places, and worrying how Dolly would take to being jumped on unexpectedly from above, I crept up. I untangled her rope and climbed frog-like on to the rock above her, and prepared to hurl myself on to the saddle. She was deeply shocked at this unexpected style of mounting, and took it into her head right then to throw a tantrum. She spun around, and sent a rock rolling over the edge of the path. That rock caught at others, and unsettled them, and then a whole landslide was crashing down, and suddenly the path was falling beneath Dolly's feet and all the Turks were wide awake.

Dolly squealed and sprang away, plunging and teetering willy-nilly along the track. Bullets whizzed past my ears, the breath of them hot across my arms.

It wasn't me tapping her on, nor the Turks that were after me, nor their gunshots, that sent her off like that, like a bullet from a pistol, head lowered and racing towards home; it was just some random snake or other small thing to which she'd taken an objection.

In any case, Dolly had decided to head for home, and on and on we went, at her finest coffee-drinking pace, until we were well out of reach of the Turks, and until my heart finally stopped pounding and we reached some place where the ground was soft and whispering with grasses, and she slowed.

I grew careless and tired. Dolly's forelock was rising gently, falling gently in the breeze, and I let my head nod, trusting her to lead us home – only because she knew there was more corn in the camp of the British Army than anywhere else in all Arabia. From time to time I would start at some whirring bird or other, and clutch at the saddle, then slowly slump back while Dolly trotted on, as indifferent to me and to the night's events as if she'd forever carried a thousand men over a thousand such miles under a thousand such stars.

We were greeted when we arrived by the smell of the frying bacon of a Tommy breakfast and all its twisting curls of smoke. Tattered and dirty and with septic sores on my skin from the sun, I found the Major, and reported to him what I'd seen of the hundred Turks that were creeping up the wadi. The Major sent off a unit to dispatch the Jackos, said I'd averted a major disaster, and that, from the look of me, I should have a sleep, and a wash.

I staggered along the camel lines and lifted the saddle off Dolly for the first time in four days. A maggoty hunk of flesh the size of a grapefruit came away with it and I gagged with horror for her. Dolly herself was above minding various parts of her body coming off with the rigging – her head, as ever, pretending to have no connection to any other part of herself. She'd grown thin on that patrol, poor Dolly. All camels lose weight on a march and every morning I'd tightened the webbing girth, but she was in poor shape now, having eaten, for the most part, only blankets and thistle and head-ropes.

I slept the rest of that day and into the early evening, then went to Dolly, as I was feeling kindly to her after her bringing me home asleep in the saddle, and parts of her being so maggoty.

Hey-Ho wasn't in his proper place but in line with the camels, and I was irritated by that, being still so tired and sore.

Captain was there beside them both, and he was lifting one of Dolly's feet, tending to the delicate pad of it. He looked up.

'She comes from the coast where the sand is soft

and white,' he said. 'Look, the pad is cracked and blistered.'

I was cross perhaps because Captain didn't ask what had happened to me after I'd been sent off alone into the dark, or perhaps because I should have tended to Dolly myself, but either way, I am ashamed to say, I snatched up Hey-Ho's rope and yanked it.

'Get him back to his proper place with the pack-animals,' I said. 'And you to yours.'

Then I went to the mess tent, and when Ballard called out to me, I joined the group around him, and took the drink held out for me. But there was no pleasure in it, for I kept seeing Captain's starting eyes. He'd looked up like a wounded animal when I'd snatched up Hey-Ho's head-rope.

I didn't sleep that night for thinking of what I'd said to Captain. For an hour or two I tossed and turned, then started to my feet at a terrible roaring and bellowing and commotion. There was a great palaver going on in the darkness somewhere, and from the roaring I knew it was in the camel lines. When I got there, all of them were slathering and foaming and mightily perturbed because of Hey-Ho, who was pattering up and down the camel line and braying, the remains of his rope trailing behind.

He'd eaten through it, and was going up and down, while all the camels were roaring and bellowing at him from one end of the line to the other, but he took no notice at all and never stopped till he found Dolly.

Captain and I came face to face there in the moonlight beside Dolly.

'Billy . . .' he said.

I bent to tighten the hobble around Dolly's ankles.

'Billy. . .'

I rose, and tightened her head-stall too, then we caught each other's gaze for an instant, and still I said nothing.

'Are you all right, Billy?'

I tightened Dolly's head-rope with another vicious twist.

'*Corporal*,' I said. '*Corporal*, to you.'

'*Corporal*? You are not all right . . .'

'I can look after myself. Now get that wretched animal back to his place.'

Captain paused, picked up the tattered end of rope, and whispered, 'Come, Hey-ho, come.'

His eyes were welling with tears as he walked towards the mess lines.

Moab (and other terrible places)

1917–1918

I'd survived Gallipoli and Gaza, I was sunburned and strong, I was a Camelier and, after Khulweifeh, a Sergeant. It meant nothing really, being made a Sergeant. Promotions came easily when there were so few of us who'd been there any time at all, but I was mighty proud of my stripes and crown and of the small difference that rank could bring; and, I am ashamed to say, it all went a little to my head and did no good at all.

When there was water and I could shave, I saw a face I didn't recognize. I'd been away from home now for over two years, and Bredicot was grown as misty as a dream. I didn't think Liza or Mother would recognize me if they saw me now, and I never stopped to think that I maybe wouldn't recognize Liza either, that she might have grown up too. I told Liza about being in the land of Herod and Pharaoh, but I never told her I was on a camel, for I still didn't like to think of Rudge's laughing, even then.

Later that same year there were a series of operations somewhere around Khuweilfeh, or maybe it was some other place. Either way, we had Jacko on the run. Exactly six weeks since Beersheba, we'd driven Jacko from Jerusalem.

We were so far apart, Captain and I at this time, and further apart every day. We Cavalry pushed on so fast that the baggage animals often took days to catch up. I'd never apologized for my behavior to Captain in the camel lines that night.

Settlement after settlement fell to us, each time the water sour with the dead camel flesh Jacko had left in the well. The Medical Officers would add chlorine and we'd fall to our knees and scoop up the filthy mix with our bare hands. Day after day, it was the same oscillating ripples of heat in the air, the same ripples of sand on the ground, the same furnace scorch of the sun, the same snakes and sinister saltwater wadis, the same throbbing and swimming in the head, sweat running down the forehead into our eyes, the same flies, hunger and thirst.

Jaw to tail, we Cameliers made a column like an ancient frieze, eight miles long, ten thousand of us, stretching over the white and scorching sand that hurled the glassy waves of heat back at our eyes till we were all panicky and babbling like fools. Dolly's hump grew smaller on that long march and the sides of her were visibly falling away, her ribs showing.

I never saw Captain at Jericho, but at Jaffa I was in a bad way and needed a friend. I asked around for him, and when I saw him, he was standing, still and unmoving, where Chips told me he would be, on the edge of the city, just standing and watching the road to the north, little Hey-Ho at his side.

'Captain,' I said.

He neither answered nor turned.

'We've got him on the run,' I said laughing, eyeing the sad caravan of carts and wagons and tin-pot things, all piled high, that crawled sadly out along that road.

He swung round to me, his eyes glimmering.

'We know,' he said steadily. 'Hey-Ho and I, we know what it is to leave like that, with all our things . . .'

'Oh, Captain,' I began – and he was looking at me, searchingly and with alarm in his eyes, but there are no words to make up for being so swinish, and I bowed my head and was suddenly crying, God help me, like a baby.

'Come,' he said. 'You are not all right, Billy.'

I *was* in a bad way. I woke that night, screaming and sweating because of the Turkish bayonets about to thrust and twist in the soft parts of my belly, and me not able to pick up my own. Captain gave me water and after a while I slept, but the Turks were creeping up on me, their bayonets glinting in the moonlight, and my own bayonet was in my hand but it was heavy as lead and I could not use it.

Captain put an arm beneath mine and led me to the medics.

'Poor food. Battle fatigue. Rest for a day and he'll be all right.'

Men medically and mentally unfit were returned every day to service, and I was just one more.

'Two days. Rest two days,' Captain said sternly to me.

I slept two nights in the first-aid area, in a blanket slung between two naked palms. The mail caught up with us there at Jaffa, and Captain brought me my mail, a birthday card from Liza with a drawing of Trumpet's field, the apple tree thick with red fruit. Liza had drawn an arrow to the apples saying she wished she could send them to the horses in the desert, who surely had none. Mother had written a wry note at the bottom too: 'Happy birthday, Billy. Still seventeen?'

I'd forgotten my birthday, the days and the weeks running as they did into one another. I took Captain's rifle, leaned out of my hammock and with the barrel end of it, wrote in the sand:

17

The numbers were a little wobbly, but clear enough. I held the rifle out to Captain. My hands shook as they held it out and my fingers jittered uncontrollably on the butt of it. That fluttering in my fingers, I told myself, was just because of the lack of sleep, because of the flies and the snakes and wretched whispering, buzzing things that kept me awake. Captain saw the rattling of my fingers on the wood. He paused, then took the rifle and wrote:

16

'Over two years,' he said, looking up and smiling. 'Two years since we were in Egypt.'

'Hey-Ho?' I asked. 'How is Hey-Ho?'

'He is tired. This is a long journey for Hey-Ho, too long.'

He looked at Liza's card.

'How is your horse? How is your home?'

'I only think of home', I answered. 'When you ask me about it, it seems far away and dream-like, sort of misty and shady . . .'

'Do you miss it?'

'I miss the shade and the rain and the oak trees, and I miss Mother's cooking . . .' And then all of a sudden I was missing it all very much, and was hollowed out with longing for it all, and it was only when Captain rose sadly, and turned to leave, that I pulled him by the arm and asked him, tentatively, what I should have asked long ago.

'Do you . . . do you ever think of *your* home?'

Captain was silent awhile.

'I remember so little – except the pancakes –' he smiled – 'but sometimes, sometimes when I see Hey-Ho, and his legs look like little sticks and his pack is three times the size of his body, and he looks sort of like a lollipop –' Captain spread his arms wide to denote the bulk the little donkey carried – 'then I remember it all . . .'

Captain came back to my hammock next morning, leading Dolly and Hey-Ho. The sight of Dolly and her great teeth right there on the edge of the medical station caused a certain amount of consternation and suddenly orderlies emerged from all corners stepping forward in alarm, but Captain said something to the orderlies and somehow in the end they allowed him to tether Dolly and Hey-Ho round a tree that was near, but not too near.

'She has a secret,' Captain said to me, and I remembered he'd said that once before, and wondered what sort of a secret a vociferous, voluble creature like Dolly could possibly keep to herself.

'Tell,' I said.

'She will tell you herself.'

Captain came and went a bit, but he left Hey-Ho there with us, and I assumed it was because he thought it would keep my spirits up to have them there for company. Dolly was quiet, though, and didn't go about any of her usual skullduggery, and after a few hours even the orderlies grew used to the strange pair standing there on the margins of the First-Aid Post.

From where I lay, I could see some of Captain's comings and goings as he went about his work. Everywhere he went, men called to him and waved and beckoned. Each time, he'd turn and wave and smile his quiet smile, and walk straight on. There were many new recruits then – young ones, that seemed to us like boys, arriving freshly every month, all spick and span and wet behind the ears – but we were neither of us drawn to them, the distance being too great if you'd been at places like Gallipoli and Gaza.

Captain spent the afternoon with me, playing cards and getting up and down to check Dolly had water and hard food, until it wasn't at all clear that it was me who was ill and not her.

I thought about the time I spent with Ballard and the others, and wondered that Captain, though so liked by all the men, had made no other friend than me. I asked him about that, as I lay there on my hammock, and he answered,

'Father told me to trust no one . . . I have you and I have Hey-Ho. That is enough.'

That evening Dolly calved, suddenly and briefly, and in the way that she did everything: looking about herself with general displeasure, with her nose high and affecting a great indifference to what was going on at the other end of herself. It was a wonder really how she'd managed the begetting of a calf, her having so little affection for any other camel. So this was the secret that Captain had guessed long before I ever would have. The syces had told Captain that Dolly was ready, that it would be now when the moon was full.

Then suddenly, there was the calf, casually dropped behind her on the sand, as though she did such things every day without noticing: a silky scruffian, a delicious furry thing, who tried to scramble to his feet and stand just as soon as he was born. The calf already had the legs of a giraffe and the ears of a kangaroo and the soft coat of a new-born lamb, but it had a smooth and rounded back which gave the orderlies such surprise that they wondered among themselves if Dolly had not managed to conceive some other species entirely. We called him Pirate, and he was a camel-calf to melt the oldest, stoniest of hearts. The hard-riding hard-living men of the Worcestershire Yeomanry came to coo at him, and even Dolly herself showed some interest from time to time; but it might have been Hey-Ho, in the end, who loved Pirate most. He thought himself a father to the little calf, they being almost eye to eye when Pirate was born, and Hey-Ho never ceased his fatherly vigilance over Pirate, even when Pirate towered over him.

Then came the biting cold of December 1917. We lost 3,000 camels that winter. We were operating in the trackless, crooked hills of Moab – a dreadful place, where the winds bit like knives, and the stone was all broken up into pointy shards. You couldn't get any wheeled transport up there, so the ammunition was loaded on to the camels and pack-horses. They were all heavily laden and Captain was anxious for Hey-Ho. Dolly had never known the like, and she bared her yellow teeth at the rain and stones, and lifted her head to tell me that she was born for better things and should not be taken to such a place. We advanced in single file in continuous, miserable rain, me dragging Dolly and shoving her over the shifting boulders. Captain and I folded little Pirate up, in the same way Mother used to fold a picnic chair, soft pads skywards, into a string bag slung over Dolly's neck, and he was happy enough there and warm.

One day the slope was so steep that we climbed only a couple of hundred yards in eight hours, slipping and sliding. Along the dizzying brink of a crumbling cliff – to my left a drop to make the stomach turn over – I coaxed Dolly on, my breath held, fingers shaking on her head-rope. On the brow of it, she teetered and swayed. Pirate swung to and fro in his bag and my own stomach swung and sloshed sickeningly inside me. Archie Pimm gasped, and Firkins cried out, but Dolly caught her balance, raised her head and took another teetering step. Those precipices would give even a cat the collywobbles and I never again want to be on the brink of one of them on Dolly: Dolly being an inconvenient, vertiginous sort of shape for going up cliffs on.

In the pitch dark and thundering rain we slithered down the steep and stony banks of the River Jordan. It was a great race, you see, to cross that bridge and get onwards, and thousands of us converged on the banks in a colossal muddle – Infantry, Artillery, demolition parties, Engineers, Camelry and Cavalry, and somewhere, too, Captain and Hey-Ho. Dolly lost her footing on that bridge and bolted, and we crossed the boiling torrent on a makeshift pontoon at breakneck speed, her pin legs slipping on the wet boards and the captive Pirate swinging to and fro, wide-eyed with horror, and all the while from the cliffs ahead the Turkish watch-fires rose and fell and coloured the swirling water red.

On the marshy far side, we pulled Dolly up with ropes around her hindquarters while she managed to look about herself in a fed-up sort of way, as if, for all the world, she'd no idea what we were about at all. It took us cavalry so long to cross the Jordan that Jacko had time to rush away and defend Amman. We had no chance really and he defeated us there, our first defeat since Gaza. We stumbled and blundered back in the dark and the mud, every man so hungry he'd cut another's throat for a tin of bully.

Then, for a long while, and well into the summer, we were stuck there in the Jordan Valley, feeling foolish, tail between our legs, while Jacko laughed at us from the other bank. It is an unholy place, the Jordan Valley, a good thousand feet below sea level, and I never want to be in such a pit again, for in the summer there, it is all choking dust, scorpions, mosquitoes, centipedes, and spiders big as your hand. They gave us quinine every morning, but men sickened and fell like flies with malaria and the heat grew to more than a hundred degrees. We had food, plenty of it, though, now that the Engineers had made a railroad, and we got things like tea from Ceylon and flour and frozen meat.

Captain, Hey-Ho and Pirate were there, and watching little Pirate grow was the only good thing about those days in the Jordan. Otherwise all we did in those tedious months was patrol and reconnaissance, reconnaissance and patrol.

I had a shelter then, a blanket rigged between two thorns. From the shade of that I watched Pirate frolic and cavort, wondering how the cantankerous colossus that was his mother had ever produced so exuberant and playful a calf, with a coat fuzzy, fleecy and white almost as a Worcestershire lamb, and his eyes soft and liquid, and with nothing stinking about his spit and drivel. Then Pirate somehow tangled up his legs, tripped and fell. He put his neat little ears back and tilted his head and looked about over the patrician hook of his nose as if to ask who could have played such a trick on him and done that to his legs. He adjusted his position so his legs were all out, and loose, and sprawling, and careless, and elegant as a whippet's.

I was sitting there under that shelter watching all this sweetness going on when Captain came up.

'Sir.' He saluted.

He'd been saluting me since I became a Second Lieutenant and I'd never told him not to because I'd told myself that that was the correct thing in the Army, and rather liked the sound of it.

For a minute or two we both watched together the sweet daftness of the calf-camel and the donkey there together. Hey-Ho brayed, and Pirate, taking this as a call to play, tried several times to rise, then hop-skipped and skittered to Hey-Ho and nuzzled his head round and took to licking his muzzle. I think Pirate really took that grey and whiskery donkey to be his mother. Hey-Ho seemed to sigh and his eyes closed as he dropped his grey and whiskery head. I held out a hand to beckon Pirate but lowered it again when I saw the shaking in it and put it on my lap where it wouldn't rattle and Captain's eyes flickered towards my hand.

'Billy . . . ?' he began.

Captain knew that I cried in my sleep, that my nights were racked with memories of Gallipoli and Gaza and every other hole I'd been in, that I saw men bend and separate as if cut in half, bodies blown apart, shallow graves and jackals and that I woke screaming and gibbering. In the daytime my temper could flare at no provocation at all back then, and I'd snarl and bite as though I were Dolly herself. I was jumpy too then – very jumpy – and the smallest thing could turn my legs to water.

'Nothing,' I said. 'It's nothing.' And I shook his hand off.

'Billy . . .' he began again, and I snapped back.

'*Sir*,' I said. 'To you.'

Captain kept complete composure and equanimity, and said, 'Sir. Are you all right?'

A corner of the blanket was lifted. I started and sprang to one side, with a lightning shock of fear.

'Bayliss.'

I leaped to my feet, breathed deeply to stop my shivering. It was only Lieutenant Sparrow.

'Bayliss. Night-time reconnaissance. Take Pimm. Depart 16.00 hours. Turks suspected to the north. All mounted bodies approaching from the interior of the country are to be treated as enemies.' He handed me a map. I saw Captain's eyes move from me to the Lieutenant and back again.

'Sir.' I nodded.

Captain watched me pack and prepare. I turned my back to hide the shaking in my hands.

'Sir. I do not think you should go. You are not well.'

I didn't answer and after a while he said, 'Sir, is it frightening out there on patrol?' It was the way he asked, so gently, when he knew I was so often frightened, when he knew that all of me was nothing but a honeycomb of fear, and because I regretted shaking him off earlier, and because I'd made him call me 'sir' like that, that made me answer him, truthfully, or almost truthfully.

'I still find the waiting the worst, when you're on your own in the dark, just watching and waiting and there are sounds and noises everywhere.'

'And in battle, sir?'

He must've known the answer to that. I never answered him, never told him that if I was on foot, I had to force myself, one foot in front of the other; that every time, there was only one thing in my head: that I must get to the next trench, get to the next trench, get to the next trench – that it was still like it had been ever since I'd landed at Gallipoli, that somehow I felt if I got to that trench, there'd be Liza and Mother and Bredicot . . . I still couldn't say any of that so I said nothing.

'Sir, I am still scared,' he said. 'I am still scared for you.'

*

The camels' feet padded softly, silently, through the sand. The night seemed to me to be thick and teeming with sound and shadow. I started feverishly at nothing at all, the twitch of a tamarisk branch bringing a cold sweat leaping to my brow. Slits of moonlight glinted like bayonets among the rocks. I imagined clusters of Turks behind every innocent stone and bush.

When we drew close to the point on Sparrow's map, we stopped. An outcrop stood in rocky silhouette against the sky. We'd have vantage from there over the gully; vantage and protection for the animals. I hobbled Dolly, and crawled forward on my belly along a sandy crack between two boulders. We lay waiting for a while, Archie Pimm a little way behind me. My tunic was wet, perhaps from the dew, and I didn't want Pimm to see my legs shaking, so I motioned him up alongside me. I breathed in and out slowly and deeply to stem the quaking. The wind drifted over us. I started with fear at each of its comings and goings. Later, when the wind dropped, the night felt strangely still, uncanny and foreboding. Each small sound was magnified. I felt I was being watched from the surrounding rocks and expected the darkness to spout with fire at any second. I strained my eyes in search of movement, my nerves and all my senses keyed to breaking point. I thought I heard whispering voices from a clump of brushwood and kept my gun trained on it, but then I heard no other sound. It was only nervous strain, the brain playing tricks and causing me to see things which weren't there, but when I looked again, the brushwood had changed shape and the leaves of it flickered as if they'd been disturbed. Everything was strange and shifting, pregnant and explosive.

'Fix bayonet,' I hissed.

'Sir.'

I heard the slight query in Pimm's tone, but Pimm probably hadn't heard the sounds I had, didn't see that the darkness was teeming and swarming. I started again – there'd been a flash of light again, moonlight on steel. I fumbled at my bayonet, almost dropped it.

'You all right, Lieutenant?' Pimm whispered, steadying it for me.

I snatched it from Pimm and set to with it again, but my hand was shaking, and as I held it to my rifle I felt beads of sweat burst on my temple. I was all fingers and thumbs and I dropped the bayonet, and it fell, spinning and flashing to the rocks below.

Then my brain was quivering in my skull, my heart beating like a drum and the night was suddenly live with movement, bullets and blades in every shadow, in every trembling leaf a band of Turks. I heard a sound from behind – something moving to the rear – they were behind, not in front – I reached for my pistol, swung my head from side to side, waved my pistol wildly into the darkness, finger jittering on the trigger.

'Don't shoot!' Pimm cried out.

Somewhere a branch moved – silvery flickerings of moonlight on leaves – I spun my pistol to the front – swung it round again to the rear – Pimm sprang to his feet, lunged at me, clutched at my hand to stay my finger.

'Don't!' he cried again.

The branch moved again – those flickerings – there must be someone in that bush – Jacko hidden there with sharpened steel – Jacko silent and creeping up.

The sound of my pistol rang out.

A figure rose from the scrub, slim arms reaching up and outward towards me. My heart stopped. The figure staggered and, in an agonizing extension of time, his legs buckled and he fell, arms still outstretched.

Everything inside me turned pulpy and wet and quivering as I stared towards the shrub where the figure had stood.

I rose very slowly, then staggered and stumbled towards the fallen figure; slowly, tremblingly, reached out, and felt the cloth wet with blood.

'Is that you . . . sir?'

That was the only time I ever saw fear in Captain's eyes.

'Oh God, what have I done? What have I done?' I cried.

Captain's breath was short and sort of pumping, like the breath of a sheep.

'Here, sir,' he said, and his voice was weak, a bubbling sound coming from his windpipe but it was his 'sir' that twisted my heart. He touched a hand to the crimson stain on his chest. His fingers fumbled at a button for a second or two, then his hand fell limply to the ground.

I rocked back and forth, crying and helpless as a baby. Pimm saw the state of me and shoved me aside.

'Sir, I'll handle this.'

He had a field dressing ready, was unbuttoning that bloodied tunic while I buried my head in my hands and clawed the skin of my arms with my nails.

'It's in his lung, sir.' Pimm's voice was grave. 'Hurry, sir. Mount, he's still breathing.'

Pimm gathered Captain up, and once I was on Dolly, he put him in my arms.

'Captain . . .' I whispered.

A small smile breached his lips, his lashes sparkled as if with dew, and he mouthed something that I think was: 'Sir . . . Look after Hey-Ho, sir . . .'

Look after Hey-Ho: the very same words his father had said to Captain as he died on the beach at Gallipoli.

'I promise,' I said. 'I promise I will look after Hey-Ho.'

PART V

SYRIA

Out of the Jordan Valley

September 1918

I galloped with him through the dawn and through the blazing morning with all the rocks blasting like furnaces into my face, and I was wild and whirling with horror when I stumbled into camp. Chips saw the limp figure in my arms, and that was the only time I ever saw him move fast, because it was him who got hold of the stretcher and called for the Major. We fell from Dolly, the two of us, almost into the Major's arms. I am not much given to sentimentality but I swear there were tears in those stern eyes when they saw Captain. He raced with Captain in his arms to the Medical Station.

When I came up, the Major tried to turn me away from the white medical tent and I tried to push him aside, but I was weak and staggering, and he led me to another white tent and told the nurses to watch over me.

I slept perhaps a whole day, and when I awoke it was with a lightning bolt, and I lurched out of that rest-tent shouting and screaming. *Where was he and what had they done with him?* They tried to calm me and told me he'd been taken back, that he was going by train to hospital. *But would he live*, I wanted to know, *would he live?* And no one could tell me, and they shook their heads and tried to take me back into that rest-tent, but I broke free and went wildly towards the horse lines, and at some point my legs bent under me, but I went on, and I was crawling on all fours, blind with tears, scratching and scraping at the ground to reach Hey-Ho.

'Hey-Ho!' I wept as I reached him. 'Hey-Ho!' He lifted his drooping head a fraction, and he brayed, just once, and the sound of it was enough to stop the heart of any man. A good animal always knows, and you don't have to say anything at all.

There's no sound in the world so sorrowful as the *haw* of a sad donkey and in Hey-Ho's *haw* there was no smile; all the running laughter it once had was drained from it. To this day I swear that donkey never brayed again, not once.

'I will look after you,' I whispered and I was begging him, on all fours, looking up to him, reaching to him with a desperate pleading.

He dropped his head. I saw the sorrow in that little donkey's eyes. He blinked and dropped his head lower, and I saw the sorry ear that lay flat and broken on his cheek, as though it had lost its cartilage at the vital point and would never stand up again. I reached up and with a forefinger traced the wavering inky line along the tip of that ear, and then I reached for the other, the one that had once stood so proudly and was now crestfallen too, the pair of them as flat as if there were no life left in him at all.

Hey-Ho would be my cross, his every dragging step a thing to twist and wring my heart. Guilt is a searing, scorching thing, a thing that fills you to your throat and chokes you. For the next few days I took to sleeping in the mule lines and kept close to Hey-Ho at all times while we waited for news of Captain, but I never once was able to look into his eyes again.

They moved us out of the Jordan Valley and up again to Amman. At Amman we were, in the unending way of the Army, reorganized, our camels taken from us to be led back across Sinai to join Lawrence's army at Akaba. They'd been no good for the country we'd just crossed, no good for the country that lay ahead.

Dolly had carried me over the scorching wastes of Sinai and into the Promised Land, carried me safely up and down the mountains of Moab, the swaying rhythm of her stride the undercurrent of my dreams on so many a night. Poor Dolly. I was too numb to feel the loss of her and Pirate. She'd at least be in the desert she loved, I told myself dully.

I rode out on Dolly, one last time, from the Jordan Valley, Pirate trotting at our side. I knew, dully, that

I'd never again ride out on a camel, nor on any so fine a friend. I'd not deserved Dolly any more than I'd deserved Captain.

Major Straker and the others bid the great beasts farewell with full military honours, with much ceremony and pomp. I stood apart from them, watching, Hey-Ho at my side. The Yeomen formed a guard of honour, all presenting arms and the camels processed between them, led by their new Gyppy syces in their blue flowing robes. Dolly herself stalked through, slobbering and slavering in her usual way, high-headed and gloriously indifferent to all the panoply and pomp. I am not sure that Dolly ever thought much of me but when I saw her go I knew that I thought the world of her. Little Pirate trotted at her side and there were tears on my cheeks then, for Hey-Ho losing Captain, losing Dolly, losing Pirate.

I was indifferent, after this, to all men, to all company but Hey-Ho's. To Hey-Ho I was bound by guilt and blood. I was issued a fresh mount, a tall gelding called Caesar, who bore my detachment with grace and quietude. There was no news of Captain. Men began to turn their heads aside when I passed.

We had to go out again, after this, to try once more to break Jacko's line and chase him north. Only this time we were going to attack on the coast where he wasn't expecting us. We'd made tens of thousands of horses out of canvas and poles and we'd leave all our tents and those dummy horses there in the Jordan Valley and creep away in the dead of night, westward to the sea. It was a good ploy and we fooled Jacko all right. While his eyes were still on our tents in the Jordan Valley, the largest mass of cavalry ever assembled grouped on the coast and broke through his line there. When we had all his line, from east to west, we would move on north. It would be a great chase and we Cavalry were to push on ahead, fast as we could, the Transport and Service Corps following behind. The night before we were due to move on, I went to Chips.

'Sir.' He saluted me, and then touched his cap to Hey-Ho in the way he'd always done, ever since Gallipoli.

'Look after Hey-Ho,' I told him. 'If I can't be with you, if I have to go on, keep Hey-Ho close to you.'

Chips gave Hey-Ho a biscuit from the store that was always in his pocket. Hey-Ho moved his head slowly to Chips's palm, and ate.

'Heart's gone out of him . . .' Chips said sadly.

'Look after him,' I repeated, irritated, not liking to hear what I already knew.

We pushed on, over the plain of Sharon, Jacko's line crumbling into terrified clusters, the roads jammed with his troops, guns, lorries, as they tried to race away before us. We covered huge distances, snatching our rest from time to time, three hours here, three hours there and we moved so fast that we were often far ahead of the support lines.

We were armed once again with our swords, and our mounts were fresh and fit. I grew reckless and wild, taunting death, firing and riding with the best of them. Each gun rattle drummed an accusation in my ears till they might bleed with guilt. I could feel the hot, whistling breath of bullets on my skin but each skimmed by me and it seemed none could touch me, it seemed my life had a sinister, grinning charm.

It wasn't until Beisan that I saw Hey-Ho again. We were resting there, having ridden eighty miles in two days or so. When the support lines came up to Beisan I galloped down the column till I saw him. Hey-Ho was limping and footsore. I was wild and sick in my head by then, a fever in my blood, caught in the Jordan Valley, but also a sickness in my mind. It wasn't a Turkish bullet that had got me, it was the poison in my blood and in my brain. I went about the camp at night with Hey-Ho, and Firkins and Merriman and the others thought me wild and strange.

The Major had commandeered a house as Battalion HQ and summoned me there. I tethered Hey-Ho at the door and stepped inside, hoping for nothing, fearing nothing. The Major-General was in there, too.

'Bayliss,' he said. 'Step forward.'

'Congratulations,' Major Straker said, smiling.

'Lieutenant Bayliss.'

A full Lieutenant. I shuddered and shook my head.

'No, sir.' I stepped back, shaking my head, 'I've enough marks on my conscience, I want none more on my shoulder.'

'Bayliss . . .'

'What happened to Captain, sir? Where is he? Where is he?'

The Major rose and stepped out from behind his desk.

'They moved him by rail . . . we don't know . . . there are no records.' He shook his head slowly from side to side. 'You must forget what happened.'

I stepped away, feeling their eyes on my back, collected Hey-Ho and turned in the doorway, putting my hand on Hey-Ho's head.

'Billy . . .' the Major called.

'Odd fellow,' I heard the Major-General whisper as I left.

Later they promoted Firkins, of all people, in my place.

Jerusalem fell. Nazareth fell. Then Megiddo, Haifa, and at Acre our taking of Palestine was through. At Semakh, Jacko and the German gunners opened fire. We formed into line and charged we could barely see at what, for the dust and the smoke. In battle I could whittle myself to a thread, and quiet the writhing of my memories. In any space or stillness the sound of choking, the gurgling of drowning lungs, would return and make the blood in me sweep and slosh like water in a bucket. At Semakh I would have poured my last breath into the fight and I was wilder there than anywhere, fighting dismounted and hand-to-hand. Major Straker rewarded my recklessness as if it were valour, and at Semakh I was awarded a military medal.

'My medal is for Captain,' I told Hey-Ho. He looked at me, heavy-lidded, slow and unblinking, his eyes going right into the heart of me. He'd had one master and would accept no other, never loving me in the way he loved Captain. He tolerated the fistfuls of thistle I brought him, but never once nuzzled me. My behaviour with him, too, God forgive me, had grown strange and erratic.

We were ordered on to Damascus, a full ninety miles to the north. The iron will of a great General travelled through Divisional Commander, Brigadiers, Battalion Commanders, to the men, spurring us northward on the prayer of victory.

Damascus was a long way for Hey-Ho; too long. The Service Corps, with all their provisions and pots and pans, moved more slowly than we Cavalry did, but Hey-Ho, so Chips told me one night after Semakh, was the slowest of the pack-animals and had begun to trip and stumble. He'd never tripped before, and I knew then that I should be with him and watch over him.

I requested the Major to authorize a transfer to the Service Corps.

He refused me.

'For the love of God, Bayliss! No.'

'Where is he sir? What did they do with him? Tell me – is he –?'

The Major shook his head, 'I know no more than you do, Billy.' He dismissed me with a sad and worried smile.

I held my horse back, staying near the tail of our line, where I could see Hey-Ho. Major Straker was under huge pressure to push on. We were much slowed by all the service lines, and any animal that slowed us down was a serious hindrance. The little silver donkey had lost heart for the battle, his spirit visibly fading. We were ordered on to Kuneitra, and before that push we were together somewhere, all of us, one night.

Chips applied to see me and said, 'He can't keep up, sir, even without a load . . . Kuneitra will be too far.'

I applied once more for a transfer.

'For God's sake, Bayliss, stop this nonsense,' was all the Major's answer.

Chips was waiting for me outside.

'Sir, they'll shoot him. They're under orders. Any animal that can't keep up . . .'

I turned and went straight back to the Major. This time he spoke, with quiet fury through gritted teeth.

'There's so few of us, Billy. . . Merriman, Tandy,

Merrick, Robins . . . All gone . . . I need you . . . you're one of us.'

I played the last card I had.

'I'm under-age,' I said. 'I wish to leave.'

'It's too late, Bayliss. You're not under-age any more,' the Major answered sharply, and I wondered that he knew.

He was hard pushed, the Major, on that race to Damascus. He knew the ties that bound me, bound us all, to Hey-Ho, but the course of the war would be determined by this race and he was subject to the Brigadier, and the Brigadier to the Major-General, and so on, and we in the ranks had no choice.

Somewhere on the road to Kuneitra next day, the Major went on ahead to reconnoitre, leaving Captain Mason to take command of our line. The Captain knew we weren't going fast enough for the General, and he was going up and down the line, harrying us all on. I could see the quaking in Hey-Ho's legs, grey-black muzzle almost to the ground, the sorry, fallen ears. He tripped and stumbled, and never, ever, had I seen that sure-footed little animal trip or stumble before. Terrified for him, I kept to the tail of the line, keeping him in my sight.

Several horses, several of the service animals, were flagging – not only Hey-Ho, but it was Hey-Ho who fell to his knees. The line behind was held up on the narrow road, units converging and muddling up, and officers were cussing and shouting. I dismounted, and Chips and I stood on either side of Hey-Ho and tried to coax him to his feet. There were two large cans on that little donkey's back, but Chips, God bless him, had left them empty.

'It's no good, sir . . .'

'I promised,' I said. 'I made a promise. At Kuneitra I will find somewhere to keep him safe . . .'

Captain Mason was forcing his way back down the line to see what was causing the delay.

'Christ, Billy!' Chips's face was streaked with sweat.

Captain Mason was hard-pressed by his own superiors, I guess, as much the Major was, but Captain Mason was a young and callow man. I saw the harried lines of his face, the pistol in his hand.

'Lift him, Chips,' I hissed, rank with fear. 'Then we'll hold him up when the officer comes by.'

Captain Mason halted his mare in front of us.

Hey-Ho's forelegs quivered and shook but we held him between us and looked the other way.

He loaded his pistol.

'No, sir,' I said to the Captain. 'No.'

'He's been with us since Suvla, sir,' said Chips.

The Captain raised his pistol.

I took a step forward, blocking the Captain's line.

'No, sir, No. No one has the right to do this . . .'

Captain Mason's arm and pistol were raised and level.

'Step aside, Bayliss, and turn your head away. I'll deal with you later.'

I stood my ground and went on, recklessly. I knew I'd be charged for this later, for insubordinate behaviour.

'You weren't there at Gallipoli,' I said. 'You never went down on your knees for water, never scooped it up with your bare hands or drank it from the ground like a dog. We depended on him for our lives . . .'

'Turn your head aside, Bayliss,' said Mason. 'And move on down the line.'

Chips grasped my arm.

'Billy,' he said. 'Billy – look – he can't breathe – he's choking . . .'

My eyes flickered for a second to Hey-Ho, then back to Mason.

'He never so much as flinched at a Turkish bullet . . . never shirked . . . not a day sick or sorry . . .'

'Bayliss. I will have no further argument. Move away and I will see you later.'

Captain Mason's arm was still levelled, and my eyes were on him, but his own eyes were on Hey-Ho, on the straining legs, the heaving flanks and streaming neck.

Somewhere further on there was a command to halt and the line came to a weary, disorderly standstill. Hey-Ho's matchstick legs were faltering and staggering and disconnected. I stayed where I was. The Captain's arm hesitated there with the pistol, the resolve in his eyes loosening.

'Billy,' Chips said, his eyes towards a horse galloping down the line in a cloud of dust. Suddenly Captain Mason's arm was knocked, and his pistol spun in the dirt of the road.

'God forgive you,' said Major Straker to the Captain. 'Any animal but this one . . .'

'Billy,' Chips whispered. 'Billy . . .'

I heard the rasping breath, and turned, and saw the slender legs quiver and fold, as though there were no bone in them.

Hey-Ho lifted his head and half reared, and gave a bark that was a cry of pain and grief. He staggered back, nostrils wide, limbs confused and dazed and all disconnected, as though they none of them belonged to each other or to him. They seemed to turn to water and give way.

'Hey-Ho!' I cried, circling his neck with my arms and looking into his eyes, eyes that were still and deep as ever, full as ever, but brimming now, brimming with the sorrow of all the centuries. He fell, and the echoes of his cry shimmered like a wraith in the dusty air above him.

Perhaps thirty miles from Kuneitra, Hey-Ho lay dead on a dirt track, his whiskery muzzle in the dust, his silver cannisters all around him, his ears askew and sort of broken. I knelt and traced with a finger the dark wavering tip of one ear, the uncertain line that I'd once imagined Captain inking in during some lonely moment of his childhood.

I closed the lids of those eyes that Captain said had seen so many terrible things.

Those few of us who'd been at Gallipoli buried Hey-Ho there on the road to Kuneitra, the pear blossom and crown badge of the Queen's Own Worcestershire Hussars beside him, our colours over him, and a pair of shining water-cans at his head. The bugle played the Last Post and we raised bayonets in a reaching, glittering arch, tip to tip, over the makeshift grave, and bent our heads to Major Straker's words.

'His stout and stalwart heart will go with him, for he was on the side of angels.'

We fired a ten-gun salute and a weary troop of infantry passing along that road to Kuneitra raised their guns and saluted, and the next troop and the next until the skies over all Arabia were ringing with the news of a certain donkey's death.

'Heart-failure,' Major Straker said later.

But it wasn't. Hey-Ho died of a broken heart.

We turned and spurred our horses on to catch up with our unit. My eyes dry and hard, my blood cold as steel, I jabbed and kicked Caesar on, chasing away the unmarked mound that will forever lie beside the road to Kuneitra.

From Galilee to Damascus

October 1918

On we went along the long corridor that joins Africa to Asia, Arabia to Europe. To the east rode the gallant Australians, to the west Lawrence and the camels, we Yeomen in the centre. I no longer recognized the face I saw in my tin mirror, all traces of boyhood blown away, didn't know as mine the coolness of my pulse.

Thousands upon thousands of horsemen stepped out beneath the swaying stars, bridles jingling, gun wheels growling. Even to my own weary, raking mind, we were an other-worldly sight, we Cavalry who had to stop our fierce and honest enemy from entering Damascus.

Sometime, somewhere, in one velvet night, a band of Turks leaped at us like wild cats. We were still fighting them when dawn fingered her way over the hills. I was wounded there, the shrapnel burying itself deep in the flesh of my arm, the pain of it welcome and blinding, red hot and scorching to the bone. They got away, but we galloped them down and caught them, weary and limping, their rifles flung away.

We halted to let the Nottingham Horse go on ahead. They had to secure the ridge before we advanced further.

'Bayliss, stop here and get that treated,' Lieutenant Sparrow said.

'It can wait, sir,' I answered, and turned away. His eyes followed me. The Nottingham Horse closed in on the ridge, one company from the right, one from the left, with precise and efficient timing. The enemy streamed away north over the hills. Lieutenant Sparrow looked at the red stain of the bandage on my arm and called for a medic.

'Sir, I'll see a medic in Damascus,' I said, and spurred Caesar on.

The Turk cavalry and infantry, several thousands of them, were perhaps six miles ahead and racing for the city. We halted for breakfast, the brass-hats giving final orders to Divisional and Brigade leaders, splitting us off into groups of four to ride down on bands of Turks more than ten times our number. I thrashed on, chasing Captain from my mind. I'd promised to look after Hey-Ho and I hadn't. I rode as though the devil were at my heels, my heart dry and cracked and blank as the ground beneath.

We drove out all before us, riding the whole of that day, spreading out across the dusty plains in a line so thin the enemy planes could find no target, their bombs falling blankly and careless plumes rising. The going was tough, the hills steep, the wadis slippery, the plains hard-baked as stone. We rode thirty-five miles, no water for the horses, our lips cracked and black. We moved so fast the telegraph could not keep up with us, news of our progress travelling ahead of us only by plane.

Lean and hardened by the mad race from Galilee, by the hard-fought days and fleeting, sleepless nights, unshaven, dusty, our eyes bloodshot, we picked our way up rocky ground to a plain that opened out, empty and level. I had no fear now of the twist of a bayonet in my flesh. Steely and ruthless I was, riding like a devil, fighting like a devil, my throat thick with dust, eyes blurred with sweat, and I was at Johnny Turk's door by the time the sun was low.

'Jacko didn't think we could move so fast!' The Major laughed, seeing the panicky stream of Turks trying to get away up the railway valley in any tin-pot thing. I saw those people being chased from their homes and whatever the right and wrong of it all was, I thought of Captain at the gates of Jaffa, and could not laugh with the Major.

'Do they know, sir?' I asked. 'Have you heard where Captain is – if he is –?'

The Major shook his head.

'No. . . They moved him to another hospital. That's all we know.' Then he looked at me and said, 'What was his name, his *real* name? It's almost impossible to trace a man here, especially if we don't even have his name.'

'Benjamin,' I said. 'Where he came from, they used to call him Benjamin.'

'Nothing else? Just Benjamin?'

'That's all he ever told me.' I answered.

Damascus lies in a semicircle of tawny hills. Its gardens are as green and lovely a place as Jerusalem or Bethlehem, and if I'd had any softness left in me, the sight of it would have been as sweet as the green fields of Bredicot. After the blistering sand and white rock of Sinai, the silvery runnels, pearly minarets, the green gardens should have given ease to my streaming, blood-raked eyes, to my twisted mind but I saw Damascus with cold, hard eyes.

There she lay before us, the oldest living city in the world. The race to take her would end tomorrow. The prize for her would be victory and peace. I would ride hard, fight hard to take her, but there would be no peace for me. For me there would always be the knowledge of what I'd done, there'd always be the memory of Captain and his Hey-Ho.

The stuttering of the machine guns and the rattle of rifles faded. We slipped from our saddles, and fell beside our horses, the gunners beside their burning guns.

A blistering lightning flash was followed by a violent percussion – an ammunition dump exploding in a terrific column of smoke, then another. Explosion followed explosion, flashes stabbing the sky, one fire-burst after another, smoke shells breaking into rainbow stars, explosives of all kinds bursting in showers of golden rain. The latticed wireless mast swayed and crashed, the power station exploded in flying shards. A drum of petrol went up, flinging up a burst of flame. The flames leaped from drum to drum. Fodder and tents went up, and all the provisions of all the Turkish forces of Syria, Palestine and all Arabia were there burning before our eyes in a monstrous pyre.

The city glowed blood-red. A roll of thunder roared from hill to hill, to and fro, and across the Arabian desert with echoes that would reverberate across the world. Lieutenant Firkins was silent, dumbfounded by the sight of so much history happening right before his eyes.

I watched till the fires stuttered and grew fitful. The eastern night put on her velvet black. The sweat was caked on Ceasar in white streaks, his flesh raw beneath the girth and saddle, head dropping. Huddled in my blanket beside him on the bare hilltop, I listened to the cries of the jackals and the sighing of the horses, and stared up into the cruel, cold stars that could see into the heart of me.

That race north took a great toll on us all, but physical exhaustion can still the twisting of the heart and, that night at least, I slept like the child I no longer was.

Dawn came and blurred the gardens in soft river mist. All the armies lay in view: on the hills the New Zealanders and their guns, the Fourth Cavalry along the road to the north, more cavalry still on the ridge beyond, other mounted divisions on the Beirut–Damascus road. There were guns and snipers in the green and pearly city, but there'd be no heart in their fight now.

We were hard-fighting, hard-riding, well armed and well mounted and at last we had the upper hand. A great and gallant army was rushing away before us.

A regiment of the Australian Light Horse formed the advance. The Yeomen moved on at a brisk trot behind, a line two miles long, laughing and shouting, arms glittering, bridles jingling. We poured in from the north, from all sides, on horse, on camel, and on foot, flooding the plain, more units joining us, minute by minute, more mounted men from all sides, and all the hoopla, all the pride and honour and razzmatazz, all ranks moving as one and before us the pearly city quivering in the green. Nerves thrilling to the joy of an open plain, Caesar danced and jigged and there *was* splendor in it all.

The sun broke across the city and amplified the glory of the day, but despite it all I shivered, feeling the dark space at my side where Captain and Hey-Ho should've been.

And when we came in sight of the Deraa road a halt was called. A pitiful rabble was fleeing along that road, a confused, chaotic stream of bullocks, carts, motor cars, lorries, wagons, limbers, camels, horses and field kitchens. I thought again of Captain at Jaffa and of journeys across snowy mountains, and then suddenly I was thinking of Bredicot and of armies chasing Liza and Mother and Francis and Geordie out, and then I no longer knew any more what was wrong and what was right.

I was at the Major's side just then, and he turned to me and said, 'It was all for this, Bayliss, all for this.'

I turned away.

You could rely on Firkins for a historical perspective and he'd clearly prepared some words and put his pipe aside for the moment: 'A proud, fighting nation brought to her knees. An empire that has held the armies of Europe at bay for centuries, now breathes her last.'

The advance was sounded. A roar rolled like a great wave along the line. I was long, long tired and there was nothing in me that thrilled to the mass of trembling horseflesh, to the pounding of hoof and the drumming of blood and muscle, and the flashing swords, and I neither laughed nor shouted with the others as we chased and harried the terrified Turks away.

We galloped through the green and silver gardens and clattered into a winding street and into a day of carnival. All the ways were thick with people, who clung to the necks of our horses, kissed our stirrups – my stirrups and the stirrups of all the men, even Firkins's. Rolling waves of song and cheer followed us, the walls lined shoulder to shoulder, everyone singing and laughing and weeping, the women hanging out their carpets, throwing flowers and sweetmeats from latticed windows and crying out a thousand welcomes. Cries were taken up and carried from street to street, in a swinging chant. They sprinkled us with rose water and all sorts, and it was like a dream, the confetti and the crying and the clapping and the laughter tumbling from the latticed windows, but there was no Captain, and the little donkey who'd travelled so far, from the place he'd once called home, through Europe to Egypt and Gallipoli, through all of Sinai and Palestine, with the boy he loved – he was not there.

A high chieftain converged with us in a small square, behind him a band of Arabs mounted on wiry, fast-stepping ponies, all silver harnesses and jingling bells. Men whispered and pointed. He was not an Arab but a blue-eyed Englishman in all that glorious oriental get-up.

'Lawrence, the soldier-scholar . . . that's Lawrence,' whispered Lieutenant Firkins, a little breathless at the sight of the great man.

Lawrence's men saw our khaki and saluted us with thundering salvos, fired at the heavens, again and again, as though to empty their magazines at the joy of an ancient city once again in Arab hands. Behind Lawrence's ponies came camels, heads high on their swaying necks, eyes hooded, unsurprised by the hysteria and the confetti in their forelocks.

Dolly?

Our camels had gone to Lawrence – where was she?

I yanked poor Caesar round, and turned him down the ranks of camels, forcing a way through the heads that bent to my stirrups, the hands that offered sweetmeats, and peaches, and grapes, the fingers that slipped flowers into Caesar's bridle. *Dolly.* I fumbled in my pockets for a date, kicked Caesar on. He snorted and danced, light on his feet in protest at the presence of so many camels at such close quarters. I pressed him on past camel after camel, all brown and run-of-the-mill sorts of thing.

Dolly! A young Arab boy, sitting higher than his companions, a bunch of grapes in one hand, a rifle, skyward, in the other, was turning into the street. I forced Caesar down against the flow of brown camels. Dolly! Tall and creamy, confetti tangled in her forelock and lashes. Ancient eyes in an ancient head, she gazed upward and over the minarets and mosques as though she'd seen such sights each day since she'd been born. For a passing second, with a lurch of feverish hope, I thought I saw too a small grey donkey with sorry ears at Dolly's side. A hand held out grapes, a head cried into Caesar's neck, clinging to his mane. I lunged for the grapes, snatched them up and shook off the man that clung to us.

Dolly! With Pirate trotting at her side, pressing against his mother, she gazing into the middle distance in her customary way. I flung myself into the press of the crowd, thrusting Caesar's reins into the nearest hands. I looked up at the boy, then took Dolly's nose rope, rubbed her bearded chin, opened my palm to her slavery lips and blew into her nostrils. She bowed her head a little to my palm, and took the bunch of grapes in one slobbery go. The young Arab boy smiled at me.

'Good camel, very good, very fast she-camel,' he said.

'She was mine,' I answered, and there was a pleading in my voice. 'Dates,' I said. 'She likes dates . . .'

His face opened into a broad white smile as he fished inside his tunic, pulling out a fistful of sticky dates wrapped in newspaper.

'I know,' he said. 'Camel love dates.'

I fed the dates and newspaper to Dolly, tears on my cheeks as I felt the rasp of her tongue on my palm and saw her great yellow teeth. The boy smiled once more, popped a date into his own mouth, and grinning fired a thundering feu de joie up between the narrow walls then tapped Dolly onward with his stick.

I was alone, hollowed out, a chasm between me and the shrieking, clinging mob. After a long while, I retrieved Caesar, his muzzle gluey with peach juice and cake.

Weightless as a shadow, I threaded my way through the ancient dreamlike streets, a lonely figure made of dust moving silently through a crowd. I was better suited to the desert, the bustle and the chanting and the singing was too vulgar, too vivid, too sharp and strident.

The fever had been in me for a while, but that night in Damascus it got me fully in its grip, flooding my veins and squeezing the strength from me. After six hundred miles of dirt and thirst and hunger, of snakes and scorpions and shrapnel, I was too dead-tired to fight the poison – either that or it was all the vigour and the life of the living that twisted a blade in me: their crying and singing, and all the fact of so many living, when gentle Captain, gentle Hey-Ho were not.

In my left arm was a splinter of metal, a sliver too slender to do much harm, only the sepsis of the wound was troublesome. They put me between crisp sheets, where breezes flitted across my damp face. I'd start and clutch with fear at the throbbing in my arm as if I might find it gone, blown off. I was sick in body and spirit, my dreams jagged, my memories twisting and whipping, screaming, scraping things, unbearable as the constant scratch of metal against a raw nerve.

At some point the splinter and septic flesh were cut out, but the fever still raged and I stayed between the whitewashed walls and the wafting breeze.

One day Straker was there in the corridor talking to Nurse. He came in to me.

'The fever's gone,' he said. 'Nurse says it's gone.'

I turned aside.

'I need you to attend a ceremony. Nurse says you can go.'

I didn't answer, not wanting to go to ceremonies or anywhere.

'You and I,' he said. 'We're all that's left.' I felt the hesitation in his friendly hand and convivial tone, saw the wariness in his eyes as he studied me.

'Why not Firkins?' I asked.

'The dysentery got him.' Straker turned to the acacia tree outside the window. 'And Sparrow,' he said.

'Captain?' I asked.

He shook his head.

'Look, Bayliss, I don't think there's any hope. You must forget what happened out there in the desert.

For your own sake, please forget.'

Later, when he led me through the scented streets of the bazaar, with its endless hawking and selling of things, he explained my duties: I was to stand behind his chair and take notes. New boundaries would be discussed, new empires drawn up, a new world established. I stood like a shadow amidst all the toing and froing of carts and vendors, the noise of the street crowding me till I felt I might scream at the horror of so much life all still going on. The Major's arm tightened round my shoulder as he steered me through the crowd, described the format for the evening, ran through my duties once more.

'It's right you should be with me, Billy,' he said again. 'We were both there from the start . . .'

Somewhere, someone shouted. There was the lash of a whip.

'They have their ancient city back, and their ancient ways,' he said, and the lines of his mouth were grim and firm. The whip cracked again, and his eyes flickered towards the sound, then flickered back to me. No horseman likes the sound of a whip. I thought of Liza and Mother and what they thought of the Arabs and their ways. The whip was lashed again. This time we both turned. Caked with dirt and dung, the criss-cross lacerations on his skin thick with flies, the animal limped on two aching paces, then stopped and hung his nose to the ground. I turned away. Straker's eyes stayed there, then shot back to me.

'Come, Bayliss,' he said quickly, taking me and turning me.

At the door of the town hall, I heard the Syrian driver crack his whip again, and I winced, as if it were meant for me, as if the skin of my own back were slashed at the stroke of it. The donkey squealed. Straker didn't turn. He looked instead, pointlessly, at the watch on his wrist.

'Come on.'

His hand reached out to mine.

'Bayliss, we'll be late.' His voice was strung taut as wire. Steering me round, he adjusted the collar of my tunic as though I were a child. He led me through a palmy courtyard where the breeze played through the fronds and through the white high-ceilinged rooms. Coffee and grapes and sweetmeats lay on silver platters.

Later, we soldier servants stood around a glittering table; seated at it were the masterminds of the most perfect campaign in cavalry history. Crystal clinked, the chandeliers glittered on candlelit faces and rich wine flowed. They talked of boundaries being drawn, of the creation of Palestine, of armistice, ranks and honours, politics, diplomacy and promotions. Troops would be moved from here to there, provisions from here to there, camels from here to there, munitions from here to . . . somewhere. I stood in the candle-shadows, behind Straker, hearing the smooth talk as thick and distorted as if through fog or water.

Firkins. Tandy. Merriman. Robins. Spade. Beasley. Merrick. Farmer. Skerret. Hadley. Carter. Sparrow.

All the men who lie under a packing-crate cross in the stone of Gallipoli, the Yeomen of Worcestershire whose rich blood will forever water the dry sand of Sinai; they weren't there.

Captain.

The gap where Captain should be beckoned and gaped, dark and vacant as an abyss into which I might fall and sink.

Sixty thousand camels must be dealt with. They'd be sent to India. All troops would be transported home, but there'd be no transport for horses, each and every one to be sold to the Egyptians. The horses who'd carried us as we slept in our saddles, whose gait had been the rhythm of our days and nights.

When we stepped out into the great square the Major was silent. We headed through the narrow streets, and the selling and all the business of the Arab world that is never done, walking side by side in silence. A horse, closely hobbled, stood at a corner, eyes clustered with flies, panniers laden with brushwood. We remained there a while beside that horse till the Major said, 'We've orders to move on to Cairo.'

'No,' I said. 'No more, I'm through . . .'

'Bayliss,' he said, catching my shoulder. 'Billy . . .'

I turned away.

'There are ghosts.' I was wild and pleading. 'Everywhere I look, I see Captain. I see him in the streets, at every corner, then I see him again in – in the night . . .'

Straker tried to take my hand.

'Billy, it wasn't your fault, what happened.'

I shook him off.

'Tell me where he is? Where did they take him?'

'I don't know . . .' He shook his head sadly. 'No one seems to know, there're no records . . .'

After that the fever in me blew up once again, frantic and billowing. Weak already, I fell ill with the dysentery that had taken so many others. I was moved to a different hospital, sent by train to Cairo.

A new nurse read from the paper of a treaty signed at Lemnos, an armistice between Britain and Turkey. She said Bulgaria was out of the game, Austria was begging for peace, Germany disintegrating. Thirteen days later Aleppo was taken, and hostilities with Germany had ceased.

'Three years,' Nurse said. 'It's three years since Gallipoli and now you've taken Jerusalem, Damascus, Aleppo, Baghdad . . .'

Somewhere a barrel organ and pianola played. The jacaranda outside my window was in bloom. Another voice answered her, an orderly perhaps.

'He's so young.'

'We both were,' I whispered, looking away. 'He was only fourteen at Gallipoli.'

They ignored me, spoke over me as they tucked in the fresh sheet.

'So many,' said Nurse, 'but none so young.'

I turned my hot cheek to the cool pillow. We'd been just boys . . .

'He screams in his sleep and covers his eyes,' she said. 'I can't make any sense of him.'

Later Nurse read to me from an English newspaper. There was a new mayor in London, a race meeting at Newmarket, trouble for the coal masters. All the tiny things of England, and all its dappled light, were paraded before me, till I could see Mother at the breakfast table, the green-and-white crockery, Liza by the apple tree with Trumpet. Nurse read a new report too, on Gallipoli, but I wasn't listening.

Probably Liza was a grown woman now, perhaps she never went any more to see Trumpet in his field.

Tears streamed down my cheeks.

'You'll soon be going home,' Nurse said brightly. 'First to arrive will be first to leave. A shipload of you, battalion strength, and a brass band playing you home to Dover.'

'He had no home,' I said. 'Captain had no home to go to.'

She put the paper down as a visitor entered the room.

Major Straker.

'Visitors have five minutes only, please. He's still delicate and mustn't be excited.'

'What I have to tell him won't help, then.' Straker's voice was hard and grim.

'Captain? Captain? What's happened? Tell me . . .'

He shook his head.

'The horses. It's been confirmed,' he said, and his head was bowed. 'About the horses. They all go, twenty thousand of them, all sold to the Gyppies . . .' He raised his head. 'I can't do that, Billy, we can't – we can't *leave* them here.'

He put a light coat over my shoulders and drove me out to the horse lines.

'We have no choice, we can't leave them here to be ill-treated,' he said to me in the motor.

'Captain?' I asked again. 'Do you not know anything at all? Tell me. Tell me what you know.'

'I don't know any more than you do. No record of him in the wounded, no record of him in the dead. I tried to trace the name "Captain" – tried to trace the name "Benjamin" – but the hospitals are bursting – there're men on the floor, in the gardens, the corridors, and not enough staff to cope, and a boy – under-age –' and with that he looked at me sharply – 'with no surname that we know, not in the regular Army – he's just not a priority . . .' Straker smiled then sadly, and looked at me, and said, 'Billy – Bayliss – if he is alive, I promise, God forgive me, I promise there will always be a place for him on any boat that takes the Yeomen home.' And we were both thinking of that last night at Suvla, and remembering.

'Help me find him, sir,' I said. 'If he's here . . . help me find him.'

He shook his head.

'Later, Bayliss, first this . . .'

We drew up. The Major turned the engine off, bowed his head a minute or two, then lifted it slowly.

I followed him, blind and numb, to the horse lines. He untethered his mare, while I stood there, blank, doing nothing. He looked at me, then untethered Caesar, too, and led them to the water. While they dipped their noble heads and drank a long draught of cool, sweet water, Straker handed me a pistol and some lumps of sugar from his pocket.

I held the pistol in my hands, staring at it. I looked out across the acres of sand and down again at the pistol.

Caesar lifted his head from the trough. We didn't ride them, nor did we even bridle them. They walked at our sides towards the palms. The Major-General turned his head as we passed and nodded gently. On the edge of the palm grove, Straker nodded to me to

241

wait, while he took his mare on ahead a little way. I waited, head bowed, unresolved and numb, weightless and tenuous as a shadow.

Caesar started at the shot that killed Straker's mare. He'd never flinched at fire before and I was shaken, almost, from the insensible, bodiless torpor I was in by his rearing and squealing; but I saw the Major's harrowed face, I saw too that he was waiting for me. I tied Caesar's old head-rope to a palm and stepped away.

I thought of Liza and her letters. Could I go home and tell Liza I'd left a good Worcestershire horse here? There was no grass, not a single primrose in the whole of Arabia. 'I will do this for Liza and this will be the last shot I ever fire. I will never again hold a gun,' I said to myself.

I raised my right arm and levelled it and tried to find some shard of ice within myself.

'Billy – sir!'

My hand stayed there, arm levelled, my finger on the trigger.

'No! Sir, no!'

I heard those words and I thought they were Pimm's. I thought it was Pimm again, calling out to me in a dark and teeming desert night, where branches moved and leaves flickered and there were sharpened blades in every bush. My trigger finger began to tremble, my arm was shaking violently, the whole of me quaking.

'Sir! No!'

The voice wasn't Pimm's. It was the madness in my brain that made me think it was Pimm, that and the poison in my veins, and the ghosts that were around me at all hours. I kept that pistol raised, kept my arm level, but I crumpled and cowered and covered my eyes and wept.

'Sir . . .'

My fingers were uncurled one by one, gently, from the handle of that pistol, then my forefinger from the trigger, and the pistol fell to the sand.

'You are not all right, sir.'

I opened my eyes. A pair of bare feet stood in the fine white Egyptian sand. And that sand – every grain of it glistened and glittered and refracted the rosy apple of the setting sun. I lifted my eyes slowly upward.

Captain.

'Sir . . .' he said.

The sky was as soft and warm as the sky over Bredicot at sundown.

'Billy,' I answered. 'Just Billy.'

Almost in the very spot where I'd first seen him, stood Captain. The palm fronds rustled above him.

'Billy,' he said, smiling. In his hand was a fistful of grapes and his arm was extended to Caesar, who whinnied for joy at the scent of them. Captain no longer wore British service dress, but on the collar of his shirt was a military medal, and beside it a tattered and faded rosette.

'I have been waiting a long time,' he said. 'I have been waiting here because I knew, sooner or later, you would come to the horses. You always go to the horses when you are sad, Billy, and I knew you would come.'

'Thank God,' I said. 'Thank God.'

He put a hand to his chest. 'I am all right. It is all right. The English doctors are good.'

'Hey-Ho . . .' I began, but I could not go on, and I dropped my head in shame.

'Hey-Ho was old, Billy, old and tired. He had come a long way, he had a long life and he was with you, he was walking beside a friend.'

AFTERWORD

The morning room at Bredicot, 1919

I found a bundle of letters, neatly ribboned, at the back of a drawer of Mother's desk, the paper torn from a note book, and covered in Straker's precise hand. Mother and Liza knew all along, you see, that I had a friendly eye on me.

Reggie Straker came by today with a gift from the Yeomen of Worcerstershire. Mother told him that having four boys – four men – she'd smiled at me – in the house was no worse than three. Geordie looked frightfully puffed up at being called a man. When Liza nagged at Straker for leaving good Worcestershire horses alone in Egypt, he bowed his head. Mother changed the subject and said it was at least a relief we hadn't bought the camels back, as it might be a trouble to have a camel about the place, and I smiled to think what short work Dolly would make of her roses and her tapestries.

Liza is making pancakes. Captain is in the field outside the window with the cow parsley and the primroses all about. In a corner of the field Trumpet and Caesar stand together. Mother, you see, took a dim view of the way the Army treated those horses after the war, and she sent Liza to Cairo to fetch Caesar back. Captain is amazed there are so few donkeys in Worcestershire. But when Straker came today, he brought one donkey with him to Bredicot. The donkey stands quietly on lollipop legs, a burden three times his bulk on his back. His cans do not clank and rattle. His gusty, smiling bark is silent. With Straker too came a camel which stands beside the donkey. She doesn't slaver and spit or go about any of her customary skullduggery in the mule lines.

There they will be forever, side by side on the mantel, looking east, each as ancient and biblical as the other: the stout-hearted donkey and the crabby, crotchety camel.

SOLDIER DOG

SAM ANGUS

'He'll always be true, faithful and brave,
even to the last beat of his heart.'

It's 1917. In the trenches of France,
miles from home, Stanley is a boy fighting a
man's war. He is a dog handler, whose dog must
be so loyal that he will cross no-man's-land
alone under heavy fire to return to Stanley's side,
carrying a message that could save countless lives.
But this journey is fraught with danger,
and only the bravest will survive.

As the fighting escalates and Stanley
experiences the true horror of war, he comes
to realize that the loyalty of his dog is the
only thing he can rely on . . .

A HORSE CALLED
HERO

SAM ANGUS

War took his hope, a horse gave him courage

London, 1940. Dodo and her little brother Wolfie do
not know what has happened to their father. A cavalry
officer, war hero and veteran of the Somme, he has gone
missing at Dunkirk. The children are evacuated to the
West Country, away from everything they know. Alone in
a high and wild land, they are taunted and bullied when
their father is accused of cowardice and desertion.

Wolfie finds an orphaned foal, names him Hero and raises
him. Together they roam the hills, finding freedom and
happiness, little suspecting the dark shadow that hangs
over them and the test that lies in store for them both . . .